Hi, I think all The Princess Diaries books are brilliant.
Whether it's fights with Lilly or boyfriend trouble –
Mia has it all. From Grandmere to Mr G (I mean Frank)
these books are brilliant – I couldn't put them down.
Rachael

Meg, YOU ROCK! The PD series was really good and it
shows how life is when you're a teenager (LIKE ME!!).
Except of course I'm not a princess. xoxoxo
Elana

These books are great, they are books you can really
relate to and they are so funny. I love them.
Krista

The first time I picked up this book, I thought, 'WOW!
This looks great!' As soon as I started reading it I just
couldn't bear to put it down! Fantastic novel, must be read.
Grace

They rock! These books are marvels! Don't stop writing.
Supuli

I think this was a great book and so do all my friends!!!!!
Actually I love all Meg's books and I think she's great!!!!!!!!
Chloe

It's such an excellent book – it's funny, interesting
and heartfelt. It always cheers me up and when I start
reading I can't stop.
Priya

What readers said about Meg Cabot's

The Princess Diaries

Fantastic!
Everything you need to know about being a princess!
Emma

MEGA GOOD!!!!! I'm telling you, if I didn't have this book
I would be living under a rock with all the mole people!!!
A total lifesaver in all areas!
Jess

I love your work, Meg. Never ever stop writing.
Girls all over the world will be deprived of one of
the all-time best authors!! :)
Steph

These books are totally brilliant! I've read every one
in the series at least four times!
Alix

I have read all these books and Meg Cabot is so totally
my fave author. I'd definitely give her more than five stars.
I love the way her books relate to you in some ways and in
others make you laugh out loud!
Naomi

I think this book is absolutely fantastic.
Every girl in England should have it.
It tells you about beauty, fashion and BOYS!
Lucy

The Princess Diaries

Meg Cabot is the author of the phenomenally successful The Princess Diaries series. With vast numbers of copies sold around the world, the books have topped the US and UK bestseller lists for weeks and won several awards. Two movies based on the series have been massively popular throughout the world.

Meg is also the author of the bestselling Airhead trilogy, the Abandon trilogy, *All-American Girl*, *All-American Girl: Ready or Not*, *How to Be Popular*, *Jinx*, *Teen Idol*, *Avalon High*, *Tommy Sullivan Is a Freak*, The Mediator series and the Allie Finkle series as well as many other books for teenagers and adults. She and her husband divide their time between New York and Florida.

Visit Meg Cabot's website at
www.megcabot.co.uk

The Princess Diaries

Seventh Heaven

Meg Cabot

MACMILLAN

First published in the UK 2006 by Macmillan Children's Books

This edition published 2007 by Macmillan Children's Books
a division of Macmillan Publishers Limited
20 New Wharf Road, London N1 9RR
Basingstoke and Oxford
Associated companies throughout the world
www.panmacmillan.com

ISBN 978-0-230-76800-0

1 3 5 7 9 8 6 4 2

A CIP catalogue record for this book is available from
the British Library.

Typeset by Intype Libra Ltd
Printed and bound by CPI Group (UK) Ltd, Croydon, CR0 4YY

For my niece, Riley Sueham Cabot,
another Princess-in-Training

Many thanks to Beth Ader, Jennifer Brown, Barbara Cabot, Sarah Davies, Michele Jaffe, Laura Langlie and Fliss Stevens. Special thanks to Benjamin Egnatz, who wrote many of the songs/poems in this book, and also fed me while I was writing it.

'The spirit and will of any child would have been entirely humbled and broken by the changes she has had to submit to. But, upon my word, she seems as little subdued as if – as if she were a princess.'

A Little Princess
Frances Hodgson Burnett

From the desk of
Her Royal Highness Princess Amelia Mignonette
Grimaldi Thermopolis Renaldo

Dear Dr Carl Jung,

I realize that you will never read this letter, primarily because you are dead.

But I feel compelled to write it anyway, because a few months ago during a particularly trying period in my life, a nurse told me I need to be more verbal about my feelings.

I know writing a letter to a dead person isn't exactly being verbal, but my situation is such that there are very few people I can actually talk to about my problems. Mostly because those people are the ones causing my problems.

The truth is, Dr Jung, I have been striving for fifteen and three-quarter years for self-actualization. You remember self-actualization, right? I mean, you should – you invented it.

The thing is, every time I think I have self-actualization on the horizon, something comes along to mess it all up. Like this whole princess thing. I mean, just when I

1

thought I couldn't possibly become a bigger freak, POW! It turns out that I'm also a princess.

Which I realize to many people does not seem like an actual problem. But I'd be very interested to see how THEY would react if every single spare moment of THEIR lives was taken up by lessons in being a royal from their eyelid-tattooed grandmother; getting stalked by the paparazzi; or attending boring state functions with people who have never even heard of *The OC*, let alone know what's going with Seth and Summer's on-again-off-again romance.

But the princess issue isn't the only thing that's put a wedge between me and my quest for self-actualization. Being the sole sane caretaker of my baby brother – who appears to have grave developmental problems, because at ten months he still cannot walk without holding on to someone's (usually my) fingers (and while it is true that he has shown markedly advanced verbal skills for his age, knowing two words, 'tuck' – truck – and 'kee' – kitty – he uses them indiscriminately for all objects, not just trucks and cats) – hasn't helped much either.

But that isn't all. How about the fact that I have been elected president of the student council of my school . . . but am nevertheless still one of the most unpopular people in said school?

Or that I've finally figured out that I do have an actual talent (writing – in case you can't tell from this letter), but I won't be able to pursue a career in my field of choice, because I will be too busy ruling a small European principality? Not that, according to my English teacher, Ms Martinez, who says I have a problem with the overuse of adjectives in my descriptive essays,

I'm ever going to get published, or even get a job as an assistant writer on a situation comedy.

Or even that I finally won the love of the man of my dreams, only to have him so busy with his History of Dystopic Science Fiction in Film course that I hardly ever get to see him.

Do you see where I'm coming from with all this? Every time self-actualization seems to be within my reach, it is cruelly snatched away by fate. Or my grandmother.

I'm not complaining. I'm just saying . . . well, exactly how much does a human being have to endure before she can consider herself self-actualized?

Because I really don't think I can take any more.

Do you have any tips on how I might achieve transcendence before my sixteenth birthday? Because I would really appreciate some.

Thanks.

Your friend,
Mia Thermopolis

PS Oh, yeah. I forgot. You're dead. Sorry. Never mind about the tips thing. I guess I'll just look some up in the library.

Tuesday, March 2, After school, Gifted and Talented Room

Bimonthly Meeting of the AEHS Student Government Officers

Meeting Called to Order

Attendance –

Present:
    Mia Thermopolis, President
    Lilly Moscovitz, Vice-President
    Ling Su Wong, Treasurer
    Mrs Hill, student government advisor
    Lars van der Hooten, personal bodyguard of HRH M.
        Thermopolis

Absent:
Tina Hakim Baba, Secretary, due to emergency retainer refitting after her little brother flushed her old one down the toilet

(Which, by the way, is why I'm the one writing the minutes. Ling Su can't, due to having 'artist' handwriting, which is very similar to 'doctor' handwriting, meaning it is actually indecipherable by the human eye. And Lilly claims she has carpal tunnel syndrome from typing out the short story she sent in to *Sixteen* magazine's annual short-fiction contest.

Or, I should say, the FIVE short stories she sent into *Sixteen* magazine's annual short-fiction contest.

I don't know how she found the time to write FIVE stories. I barely had time to write ONE.

Still, I think my story, 'No More Corn!', is pretty good. I mean, it has everything a short story SHOULD have in it: Romance. Pathos. Suicide. Corn.

Who could ask for more?)

Motion to Approve the Minutes from 15 February Meeting: APPROVED

President's Report: 'My request that the school library remains open on weekends for the use of study groups was met with considerable resistance by school administration. Concerns raised were: cost of overtime for librarian, as well as cost of overtime for school security guard at entrance to check IDs and make sure people entering were, in fact, AEHS students, and not just random homeless people off the streets.'

Vice-President's Response: 'The gym is kept open on the weekends for sports practices. Surely the security guard could check IDs of both student athletes and students who actually care about their grades. Also, don't you think even a moderately intelligent security

5

	guard could tell the difference between random homeless people and AEHS students?'
President's Response to Vice-President's Response:	'I know. I mentioned this. Principal Gupta then reminded me that the athletics budget was determined some time ago, and that there is no weekend library budget. Also that the security guards were mainly hired for their size, not their intelligence.'
Vice-President's Response to President's Response:	'Well then, maybe Principal Gupta needs to be reminded that the vast majority of students at Albert Einstein High are not involved in sports, need that extra library time, and that the budget needs to be reviewed. *And* that size isn't everything.'
President's Response to the Response of the Vice-President's Response to my previous statement:	'Duh, Lilly, I did. She said she'd look into it.'

(Why does Lilly have to be so adversarial during these meetings? It makes me look like I don't have any authority whatsoever in front of Mrs Hill.

I really thought she was over that whole thing about me not stepping down from office so that SHE could be President. I mean, that was MONTHS ago, and she seemed to forgive me once I got my dad to go on her TV show so she could interview him about European immigration policies.

And OK, it didn't give her the ratings bounce she'd been hoping for.

But *Lilly Tells It Like It Is* is still the most popular public access programme on Manhattan cable television – after that one with the Hell's Angel who shows you how to cook over an exhaust pipe, I mean – even if those producers who optioned her show still haven't managed to sell it to any major networks.)

Vice-President's Report:	'The recycling bins have arrived and have been placed beside every regular trash can throughout the school. These are specialized bins that are divided into three sections – paper, bottles and cans, with a built-in mechanized crusher on the can side. Student use has been high. There is, however, a small problem with the stickers.'
President's Response:	'What stickers?'
Vice-President's Response to President's Response:	'The ones across the lids of the recycling bins that say *Paper, Cans and Battles*.'

President's Response to Vice-President's Response:	'They say *Paper, Cans and BOTTLES*, not *Battles*.'
Vice-President:	'No they don't. See?'
President:	'OK. Who proofed the stickers?'
Vice-President:	'That would have been the secretary. Who isn't here.'
Treasurer:	'But it isn't Tina's fault, she's been super-stressed about midterms.'
President:	'We need to order new stickers. *Paper, Cans and Battles* is unacceptable.'
Treasurer:	'We don't have the money to order new stickers.'
President:	'Contact the vendor who supplied the stickers and inform them that they made a mistake that needs to be rectified immediately, and that because it was THEIR mistake there should be no charge.'
Vice-President:	'Excuse me, Mia, but are you writing the minutes of this meeting in your JOURNAL?'

President:	'Yes. So what?'
Vice-President:	'So don't you have a special student government notebook?'
President:	'Yes. But I sort of lost it. Don't worry, I'm going to transcribe the minutes into my computer once I get home. I'll give you all printouts tomorrow.'
Vice-President:	'You LOST your student government notebook?'
President:	'Well, not exactly. I mean, I have a pretty good idea where it is. It's just not accessible at this time.'
Vice-President:	'And why would that be?'
President:	'Because I left it in your brother's dorm room.'
Vice-President:	'What were you doing with the student government notebook in my brother's dorm room?'
President:	'I was just visiting him, OK?'
Vice-President:	'Was that ALL you were doing? Just VISITING him?'

President:	'Yes. Madame Treasurer, we are ready for your report now.'

(OK, seriously. What's with the, *Was that ALL you were doing?* You so know she was talking about S-E-X. And in front of Mrs Hill too! As if Lilly doesn't know perfectly well where Michael and I stand on *that* subject!

Could it be that maybe she's nervous about 'No More Corn!' being better than any of her stories? No, that's not possible. I mean, 'No More Corn!' IS about a sensitive young loner who becomes so distressed over the alienation he feels at the expensive Upper East Side prep school his parents send him to, as well as that of the school cafeteria's insistence on putting corn in the chilli, ignoring his frequent requests to them not to do so, that he eventually jumps in front of the F train.

But is this really a better plot than any of the ones in Lilly's stories, which are all about young men and women coming to terms with their sexuality? I don't know.

I *do* know that *Sixteen* magazine doesn't tend to publish stories with explicit sex scenes in them. I mean, it has articles about birth control and testimonials from girls who got STDs or had unwanted pregnancies or got sold into white slavery or whatever.

But it never picks stories with stuff like that in it for its fiction contest.

When I mentioned this to Lilly though, she said they would probably make an exception if the story was good enough, which hers definitely are – according to her, anyway.

I just hope Lilly's expectations aren't TOO unrealistic. Because, OK, one of the first rules of fiction is to write what you know, and I have never been a boy, hated corn, or felt alienated enough to jump in front of an F train.

But Lilly's never had sex, and all FIVE of her stories have sex in them. In one of them, the heroine has sex with a TEACHER. You KNOW that's not written from personal experience. I mean, except for Coach Wheeton, who is now engaged to Mademoiselle Klein and wouldn't even LOOK at a student, there isn't a single male teacher in this school anyone could remotely consider hot.

Well, anyone except my mom, of course, who apparently found Mr G's alleged hotness – EW – irresistible.)

Treasurer's Report: 'We have no money left.'

(Wait. WHAT DID LING SU SAY????)

11

Tuesday, March 2, the Plaza, Princess Lessons

Well, that's it then. The student government of Albert Einstein High is broke.

Busted.

Bankrupt.

Tapped out.

We're the first government in the history of Albert Einstein High School to have run through their entire budget in only seven months, with three more still to go.

The first government ever not to have enough money to rent Alice Tully Hall at Lincoln Center for the senior class's commencement ceremony.

And it's apparently all my fault, for appointing an artist as treasurer.

'I told you I'm no good with money!' was all Ling Su kept repeating, over and over again. 'I told you not to make me be treasurer! I told you to make Boris treasurer! But you wanted it to be all about Girl Power. Well, this girl is also an artist. And artists don't know anything about balance sheets and fund revenues! We have more important things on our minds. Like making *art*, to stimulate the mind and senses.'

'I knew we should have made Shameeka treasurer,' Lilly groaned. Several times. Even though I reminded her, repeatedly, that Shameeka's dad told her she is only allowed one extra-curricular activity per semester, and she'd already chosen cheerleading over student governing in a decision sure to haunt her in her quest to be the first African-American woman to be appointed to the Supreme Court.

The thing is, it really isn't Ling Su's fault. I mean, *I'm* the president. If there is one thing I've learned from this princess business, it's that with sovereignty comes responsibility: you can delegate all you want, but, ultimately, YOU're the one who is going to pay the price if something goes awry.

I should have been paying attention. I should have been more on top of things.

I should have put the kibosh on the uber-expensive bins. I should have just made them get the regular blue ones. It was my idea to go for the ones with the built-in crusher.

WHAT WAS I THINKING??? Why didn't anyone try to stop me????

Oh my God. I know what this is!

It is my own personal presidential Bay of Pigs.

Seriously. We learned all about the Bay of Pigs in World Civ – where a group of military strategists back in the nineteen sixties came up with this plan to invade Cuba and overthrow Castro, and talked President Kennedy into agreeing to it, only to get to Cuba and find out they were outnumbered and also that no one had checked to make sure the mountains they were supposed to flee into for safety were actually on that side of the island (they weren't).

Many historians and sociologists have blamed the Bay of Pigs on an incidence of groupthink, a phenomenon that occurs when a group's desire for unanimity makes them reluctant to actually check their facts – like when NASA refused to listen to the engineers' warnings about the space shuttle *Challenger*, because they were so adamant about launching it by a certain date.

This is clearly EXACTLY what went on with the recycling bins.

Mrs Hill – who, if you really think about it, could be

called a groupthink enabler . . . I mean, she didn't exactly do a whole lot to try to stop us. The same could be said for Lars, for that matter, although ever since he got his new Sidekick he hardly ever pays attention in class anyway – refused to offer any workable solutions to the situation, such as a loan of the five grand we're missing.

Which, if you ask me, is a cop-out, given that, as our advisor, Mrs Hill is at least partly responsible for this debacle. I mean, yes, I am president, and ultimately the responsibility lies with me.

Still, there is a *reason* we have an advisor. I am only fifteen years and ten months old. I should not have to shoulder the burden for ALL this. Mrs Hill should take SOME of the responsibility. Where was she when we blew our entire annual budget on top-of-the-line recycling bins with built-in crushers?

I'll tell you where: fuelling her American-flag-embroidered sweater addiction by watching the Home Shopping Network in the Teacher Lounge and paying absolutely no attention, that's where!

Oh, great. Grandmere just yelled at me.

'Amelia, are you paying the slightest bit of attention to what I'm saying, or am I just speaking to myself?'

'Of course I'm paying attention, Grandmere.'

What I *really* need to do is start paying attention more in my economics class. Then maybe I might learn how to hang on to my money a little better.

'I see,' Grandmere said. 'What was I saying then?'

'Um. I forgot.'

'John Paul Reynolds-Abernathy the Fourth. Have you ever heard of him?'

14

Oh, God. Not this again. Because Grandmere's latest thing? She's buying waterfront property.

Only of course Grandmere couldn't be happy just to own *ordinary* waterfront property. So she's buying an island.

That's right. Her own island.

The island of Genovia, to be exact.

The real Genovia isn't an island, but the one Grandmere is buying is. An island, I mean. It's off the coast of Dubai, where this construction company has made a bunch of islands, clustered together into shapes you can see all the way up in the space shuttle. Like they made a couple of island clusters shaped like palm trees, called The Palm.

Now they're making one called The World. There are islands shaped like France and South Africa and India and even like New Jersey, which, when viewed from the sky, end up looking just like a map of the world, like this:

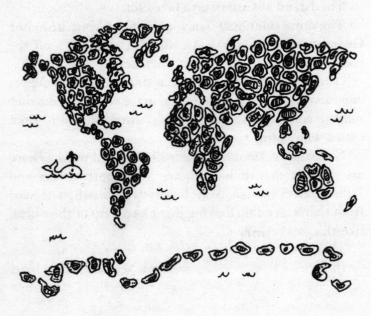

The World at Dubai
by Mia Thermopolis

Key:
island containing villa, pool, etc.
sandy beach around island

= ocean waves

= whale (not drawn to scale)

Obviously, the islands are not built to scale. Because then the island of Genovia would be the size of my bathroom. And India would be the size of Pennsylvania. All the islands are basically the same size – big enough to put a humongous estate with a couple of guest houses and a pool on – so people like Grandmere can buy an island shaped like the state or country of their choice, and then live on it, just like Tom Hanks did in the movie *Castaway*.

Except that he didn't do it by choice.

Plus his island didn't have a fifty-thousand-square-foot villa on it with a state-of-the-art security system and central air and a pool with a waterfall in it, like Grandmere's will.

There's just one problem with Grandmere's island: she's not the only bidder.

'John Paul Reynolds-Abernathy the Fourth,' she said again, all urgently. 'Don't tell me you don't know him. He goes to your school!'

'He goes to my school? But didn't you say he's bidding on the faux island of Genovia? That seems kind of hard to believe.' I mean, I know I have the smallest allowance of anyone at AEHS, since my dad is worried about me morphing into someone like Lana Weinberger, who spends all her money bribing bouncers to let her into clubs she's not old enough to get into legally yet (her rationale is that Lindsay Lohan does it, so why can't she? Plus, Lana also has her own American Express card that she uses for everything – from lattes at Ho's Deli to G-strings at Agent Provocateur – and her dad just pays the bill every month. Lana is so LUCKY).

But still. Someone getting enough allowance to buy his own ISLAND?

'Not the boy who goes to your school,' Grandmere said tiredly when I remarked on this. 'His FATHER.' Grandmere's eyelids, with their tattooed black liner, have squinted together, always a bad sign. 'John Paul Reynolds-Abernathy the THIRD is bidding against me. His SON goes to your school. He is a grade ahead of you. Surely you know him. Apparently, he has theatrical ambitions – not unlike his father, who is a cigar-chomping, foul-mouthed producer.'

'Sorry, Grandmere. I don't know any John Paul Reynolds-Abernathy the Fourth. And I actually have something a little more important to worry about than whether or not you get your island,' I informed her. 'The fact is, I'm broke.'

Grandmere brightened. She loves talking about money. Because that often leads to talking about shopping, which is her favourite hobby, besides drinking Sidecars and smoking. Grandmere is happiest when she can do all three at the same time. Sadly for her, with what she considers to be the fascist new smoking regulations in New York City, the only place she can smoke, drink and shop at the same time is at home, on the Net.

'Is there something you want to buy, Amelia? Something a little more fashionable than those hideous combat boots you continue to wear, despite my assurances that they do not flatter the shape of your calves? Those lovely snakeskin Ferragamo loafers I showed you the other day, perhaps?'

'I'm not PERSONALLY broke, Grandmere,' I said. Although actually I am, since I only get twenty dollars a week allowance and out of that I have to pay for all my entertainment needs, and so my entire allowance can be wiped out by a single trip to the movies, if I splurge on ginkgo biloba rings AND a soda. God forbid my dad should offer ME an American Express card.

Except that, judging by what happened with the recycling bins, I guess he's probably right not to trust me with an unlimited line of credit.

'I mean the student government of Albert Einstein High School is broke,' I explained. 'We went through our entire budget in seven months, instead of ten. Now we're in big trouble, because we're supposed to pay for the rental of Alice Tully Hall for the seniors' commencement ceremony in June. Only we can't, because we have no money whatsoever. Which means Amber Cheeseman, this year's valedictorian, is going to kill me, most likely in a long and extremely painful manner.'

In confiding this to Grandmere, I knew I was taking a certain amount of risk. Because the fact that we're broke is this huge secret. Seriously. Lilly, Ling Su, Mrs Hill, Lars and I all swore on pain of death we wouldn't tell anybody the truth about the student government's empty coffers until we absolutely can't avoid it any more. The last thing I need right now is an impeachment trial.

And we all know Lana Weinberger would leap at any chance to get rid of me as student body leader. LANA's dad would fork out over five grand without batting an eyelid if he thought it would help his precious baby daughter.

MY relatives? Not so much.

But there's always the chance – remote, I know – that Grandmere might come through for me somehow. She's done it before. I mean, for all I know, maybe she and Alice Tully were best friends back in college. Maybe all

Grandmere has to do is make a phone call, and I can rent Alice Tully Hall for FREE!!!!

Only Grandmere didn't look as if she was about to make any phone calls on my behalf any time soon. Especially when she started making tsk-tsking noises with her tongue.

'I suppose you spent all the money on folderols and gewgaws,' she said, not entirely disapprovingly.

'If by folderols and gewgaws,' I replied – I wondered if these were real words or if she'd suddenly begun speaking in tongues, and if so, should I call for her maid? – 'you mean twenty-five high-tech recycling bins with individual compartments for paper, cans and bottles, with a built-in crushing device for the can part, not to mention three hundred electrophoresis kits for the bio lab, none of which I can return because, believe me, I already asked, then the answer is yes.'

Grandmere looked very disappointed in me. You could tell she considered recycling bins a big waste of money.

And I didn't even MENTION the whole *cans and battles* sticker thing.

'How much do you need?' she asked in a deceptively casual voice.

Wait. Was Grandmere about to do the unthinkable – float me a loan?

No. Not possible.

'Not much,' I said, thinking this was WAY too good to be true. 'Just five grand.' Actually, five thousand, seven hundred and twenty-eight dollars, which is how much Lincoln Center charges campuses for the use of Alice Tully Hall, which seats a thousand. But I wasn't about to quibble. I could raise the seven hundred and twenty-eight dollars somehow, if Grandmere was willing to fork out the five thousand.

But alas. It *was* too good to be true.

'Well, what do schools in your situation do when they need to raise money fast?' Grandmere wanted to know.

'I don't know,' I said. I couldn't help feeling defeated. Also, I was lying (so what else is new?), because I knew perfectly well what schools in our situation did when they needed to raise money fast. We'd already discussed it, at length, during the student government meeting, after Ling Su's shocking revelation about the state of our bank account. Mrs Hill hadn't been willing to give us a loan (it's doubtful she even *has* five grand socked away somewhere. I swear I've never seen her wear the same outfit twice. That's a lot of Quacker Factory tunic sweaters on a teacher's salary), but she'd been more than willing to show us some candle catalogues she had lying around.

Seriously. That was her big suggestion. That we sell some candles.

Lilly just looked at her and went, 'Are you suggesting we open ourselves up to a nihilistic battle between the haves and the have-mores, a la Robert Cormier's *The Chocolate War*, Mrs Hill? Because we all read that in English class, and we know perfectly well what happens when you dare to disturb the universe.'

But Mrs Hill, looking insulted, said that we could have a contest to see who was able to sell the most candles without experiencing a complete breakdown in social mores or any particular nihilism.

But when I looked through the candle catalogue and saw all the different scents – Strawberries 'n' Cream!

21

Cotton Candy! Sugar Cookie! – and colours you could buy, I experienced a secret nihilism all my own.

Because, frankly, I'd rather have the senior class do to me what Obi Wan Kenobi did to Anakin Skywalker in *Revenge of the Sith* (i.e. cut off my legs with a light sabre and leave me to burn on the shores of a lava pit) than knock on my neighbour Ronnie's door and ask her if she'd be interested in buying a Strawberries 'n' Cream candle, moulded in the *actual shape of a strawberry*, for nine ninety-five.

And, trust me, the senior class is CAPABLE of doing to me what Obi Wan did to Anakin. Especially Amber Cheeseman, who is this year's senior class valedictorian, and who, even though she is much shorter than me, is a hapkido brown belt and could easily pound my face in. If she stood on a chair, that is, or had someone to hold her up so she could reach me.

It was at that point in the student government meeting that I was forced to say, queasily, 'Motion to adjourn,' a motion which was fortunately unanimously passed by all in attendance.

'Our advisor suggested we sell candles door to door,' I told Grandmere, hoping she'd find the idea of her granddaughter peddling wax fruit replicas so repellent she'd throw open her chequebook and hand over five thousand smackers then and there.

'Candles?' Grandmere DID look a bit disturbed.

But for the wrong reason.

'I would think *candy* would be much easier to unload on the unsuspecting hordes in the office of a parent of the typical Albert Einstein High School student,' she said.

She was right, of course – although the operative

word would be TYPICAL. I can't really see my dad, who's in Genovia at the moment, since Parliament's in session, passing around a candle sales form and going, *Now, everyone, this is to raise money for my daughter's school. Whoever buys the most candles will get an automatic knighthood.*

'I'll keep that in mind,' I said. 'Thanks, Grandmere.'

Then she went off on John Paul Reynolds-Abernathy the Third again, and how she's planning on hosting this huge charity event a week Wednesday to raise money in support of Genovian olive farmers (who are striking to protest new EU regulations that allow supermarkets to wield too much influence over prices), to impress the designers of The World, as well as all the other bidders, with her incredible generosity (who does she think she is, anyway? The Genovian Angelina Jolie?).

Grandmere claims this will have everyone BEGGING her to live on the faux island of Genovia, leaving poor John Paul Reynolds-Abernathy the Third out in the cold, yadda yadda yadda.

Which is all very well for Grandmere. I mean, she'll soon have her own island to run away to. Where am *I* going to hide from the wrath of Amber Cheeseman when she finds out she'll be giving her commencement address not from a podium on the stage of Alice Tully Hall, but in front of the salad bar at the Outback Steakhouse on West 23rd Street?

Tuesday, March 2, the Loft

Just when I thought my day couldn't possibly get any worse, Mom handed me the mail as I walked in the door.

Normally I like getting mail. Because normally I receive fun stuff in the mail, like the latest edition of *Psychology Today*, so I can see what new psychiatric disorder I might have. Then I have something besides whatever book we're doing in English class (this month: *O Pioneers!* by Willa Cather. Yawn) to read in the bathtub before I go to sleep.

But what my mom gave me when I walked through the door tonight wasn't fun OR something I could read in the bathtub. Because it was way too short.

'You got a letter from *Sixteen* magazine, Mia!' Mom said all excitedly. 'It must be about the contest!'

Except that I could tell right away there was nothing to get excited about. I mean, that envelope *clearly* contained bad news. There was so obviously only one sheet of paper inside the envelope. If I had won, surely they'd have enclosed a contract, not to mention my prize money, right? When T. J. Burke's story about his friend Dex's death-by-avalanche got published in *Powder* magazine in 'Aspen Extreme', they sent him the ACTUAL magazine with his name emblazoned on the front cover. That's how he found out he'd got published.

The envelope my mom handed me clearly did not contain a copy of *Sixteen* magazine with my name emblazoned on the front cover, because it was much too thin.

'Thanks,' I said, taking the envelope from my mom and hoping she wouldn't notice that I was about to cry.

'What does it say?' Mr Gianini wanted to know. He was at the dining table, feeding his son bits of hamburger, even though Rocky only has two teeth, one on top and one on the bottom, neither of which happen to be molars.

It doesn't seem to make any difference to anyone in my family, however, that Rocky doesn't actually have the ability to chew solid food yet. He refuses to eat baby food – he wants to eat either what we or Fat Louie are eating – and so he eats whatever my mom and Mr G are having for dinner, which is generally some meat product, and probably explains why Rocky is on the ninety-ninth percentile in size for his age. Despite my urgings, Mom and Mr G insist on feeding Rocky an unmitigated diet of things like General Tso's chicken and beef lasagne, simply because he LIKES them.

As if it is not bad enough that Fat Louie will eat only Chicken and Tuna Flaked Fancy Feast. My little brother is turning out to be a carnivore as well.

And one day will doubtless grow up to be as tall as Shaquille O'Neal due to all the harmful antibiotics with which the meat industry pumps its products before it slaughters them.

Although I fear Rocky will also have the intellect of Tweety Pie, because, despite all of the Baby Mozart videos I have played for him, and the many, many hours I have spent reading such classics as Beatrix Potter's *Peter Rabbit* and Dr Seuss's *Green Eggs and Ham* aloud to him, Rocky doesn't show any signs of interest in anything except throwing his dummy very hard at the wall; stomping around the loft (with a pair of hands – usually mine – to hold him upright by the back of his OshKoshes . . . a practice which, by the way, is starting to cause me severe lower back pain); and shrieking 'Tuck!' and 'Kee!' in as loud a voice as possible.

Surely these can only be considered signs of severe social retardation. Or Asperger's syndrome.

Mom, however, assures me Rocky is developing normally for a nearly one-year-old, and that I should calm down and stop being such a baby-licker (my own mother has now adopted the term Lilly coined for me).

In spite of this betrayal, however, I remain hyper-alert for signs of hydrocephalus. You can never be too careful.

'Well, what's it say, Mia?' my mom wanted to know, about my letter. 'I wanted to open it and call you at your grandmother's to give you the news, but Frank wouldn't let me. He said I should respect your personal boundaries and not open your mail.'

I threw Mr G a grateful look – hard to do while trying not to cry – and said, 'Thanks.'

'Oh, please,' my mom said, sounding disgusted. 'I gave birth to you. I nursed you for six months. I should be able to read your mail. What's it say?'

So with trembling fingers, I tore open the envelope, knowing, as I did so, what I'd find inside.

No big surprise, the single sheet of typed paper said:

Sixteen magazine
1440 Broadway
New York, NY 10018

Dear Writer

Thank you for your submission to Sixteen magazine. While we have chosen not to publish your story, we appreciate your interest in our publication.

Yours faithfully
Shonda Yost
Fiction Editor

Dear Writer! They couldn't even be bothered to type out my name! There was no proof at all that anyone had even READ 'No More Corn!', let alone given it any kind of meaningful consideration!

I guess my mom and Mr G could tell I didn't like what I was seeing, since Mr G said, 'Gee, that's tough. But you'll get 'em next time, tiger.'

'Tuck!' was all Rocky had to say about it, as he hurled a piece of hamburger at the wall.

And my mom went, 'I've always thought *Sixteen* magazine was demeaning to young women, as it's filled with images of impossibly thin and pretty models that can only serve to legitimize young girls' insecurities about their own bodies. And besides, their articles are hardly what I'd call informative. I mean, who CARES about which kind of jeans better fit your body type, low rise or ultra rise? How about teaching girls something useful, like that even if you Do It standing up, you can still get pregnant.'

Touched by my parents' – and brother's – concern, I said, 'It's OK. There's always next year.'

Except that I doubt I'll ever write a better story than 'No More Corn!'. It was this total one-shot deal, inspired by the touching sight of the Guy Who Hates It When They Put Corn In The Chilli sitting in the AEHS cafeteria picking corn out of his chilli, kernel by kernel, with the saddest look I have ever seen on a human being's face. I will never witness anything that moving ever again. Except for maybe the look on Tina Hakim Baba's face when she found out they were cancelling *Joan of Arcadia*.

I don't know who wrote whatever *Sixteen* considers the winning entry, and I honestly don't mean to brag, but

27

her story CAN'T be as compelling and gripping as 'No More Corn!'.

And she CAN'T possibly love writing as much as I do.

Oh, sure, maybe she's *better* at it. But is writing as important to her as BREATHING, the way it is to me? I sincerely doubt it. She's probably home right now, and her mother's going, 'Oh, Lauren, this came in the mail for you today,' and she's opening her PERSONALIZED letter from *Sixteen* magazine and going through her contract and being all, 'Ho hum, another story of mine is getting published. As if I care. All I *really* want is to make the cheerleading squad and for Brian to ask me out.'

See, I care MORE about writing than I do about cheerleading. Or Brian.

Well, OK, not more than I care about Michael. Or Fat Louie. But close.

So now stupid, Brian-loving Lauren is going around, being all, 'La, la, la, I just won *Sixteen* magazine's fiction contest, I wonder what's on TV tonight,' and not even caring that her story is about to be read by a million people, not to mention the fact that she's going to get to spend the day shadowing a real live editor and see what it's like in the busy, fast-paced world of hard-hitting teen journalism –

Unless Lilly won.

OH MY GOD. WHAT IF LILLY WON?????

Oh, Dear Lord in Heaven. Please don't let Lilly have won *Sixteen* magazine's fiction contest. I know it's wrong to pray for things like that, but I am begging you, Lord, if you exist, which I'm not sure you do because you let them cancel *Joan of Arcadia* and send that mean rejection letter to me, DO NOT LET LILLY HAVE WON *SIXTEEN* MAGAZINE'S FICTION CONTEST!!!!!!!

Oh my God. Lilly's online. She's IMing me!

```
WomynRule: POG, did you hear from 16 mag 2day?
```

Oh God.

```
FtLouie:   Um. Yes. Did you?
>
WomynRule: Yes. I got the lamest rejection
           letter. FIVE of them, to be exact.
           You can tell they didn't even READ
           my stuff.
```

Thank you, God. I believe in you now. I believe, I believe, I believe. I will never fall asleep during Mass in the Royal Genovian Chapel again, I swear. Even though I definitely don't agree with you about that whole original sin thing because that was NOT Eve's fault, that talking snake tricked her and, oh yeah, I think women should be allowed to be priests, and priests should be allowed to get married and have kids because, hello, they'd make way better parents than a lot of people, such as that lady who left her baby in the car outside the convenience mart with the motor running while she played video poker and someone stole her car then threw the baby out the window (the baby was OK because he was in a protective car seat that bounced, which is why I made Mom and Mr G buy that brand for Rocky even though he screams like his skin is on fire every time they try to stick him in it).

Still. I believe. I believe. I believe.

```
FtLouie:      Same here. Well, I mean, I got one
              letter. But mine was a rejection
              too.
>

WomynRule:    Well, don't take it too personally,
              POG. This is probably only the first
              of many rejections you'll be
              receiving over the years. I mean,
              if you really want to be a writer.
              Don't forget, almost every Great
              Book that exists today was rejected
              by some editor somewhere. Except
              maybe like the Bible. Anyway, I
              wonder who won.
>

FtLouie:      Probably some stupid girl named
              Lauren who would rather be on the
              cheerleading squad or have a guy
              named Brian ask her out and
              couldn't care less that she's soon
              to be a published author.
>

WomynRule:    Um . . . OK. Are you feeling all
              right, Mia? You're not taking this
              rejection thing too seriously, are
              you? I mean, it's only *Sixteen* maga-
              zine, not the *New Yorker*.
>

FtLouie:      I'm fine. But I'm probably right.
              About Lauren. Don't you think?
>

WomynRule:    Uh, yeah, sure. But listen, all of
```

> this has given me a totally great idea.

OK, when Lilly says she's got a totally great idea, it so never is. A great idea, I mean. Her last great idea was that I run for sophomore class president, and look how that turned out. And don't even get me started about the time in the first grade when she threw my Strawberry Shortcake doll on to the roof of the Moscovitzes' country house outside Albany to see if squirrels would be attracted to her very-berry scent and gnaw on her vinyl face.

```
WomynRule: Are you still there?
>
FtLouie:   I'm here. What's your idea? And no,
           you are not throwing Rocky on to
           any rooftops, no matter how inter-
           ested you are in what the squirrels
           might do to him.
>
WomynRule: What are you talking about? Why
           would I throw Rocky on to a roof?
           My idea is that we start our OWN
           magazine.
>
FtLouie:   What?
>
WomynRule: I'm serious. We start our own mag-
           azine. Not a stupid one about
           French kissing and Hayden
           Christensen's abs, like Sixteen
           magazine, but a literary magazine,
```

like *Salon.com*. Only not online.
And for teens. This will kill two
birds with one stone. One, we can
get published. And two, we can sell
copies and make back the five grand
we need to rent Alice Tully Hall
and keep Amber Cheeseman from
killing us.

\>

FtLouie: But, Lilly. To start our own magazine, we need money. You know. To
pay for printing and stuff. And we
don't have any money. That is the
problem. Remember?

God. I may only be getting a C minus in Economics, but
even I know that to start a business, you need some cap-
ital. I mean, I've seen *The Apprentice*, for God's sake.

Also, I sort of like seeing Hayden Christensen's abs in
Sixteen every month. I mean, it makes my subscription
worth it.

WomynRule: Not if we get Ms Martinez to be our
advisor and she lets us use the
school photocopier.

Ms M! I couldn't believe Lilly would bring up the M word
with me. Ms Martinez, my Honours English teacher, and
I do NOT see eye to eye where my writing career is concerned. I mean, she's loosened up a little since the whole
incident at the beginning of the school year where she
gave me a B.

But not by much.

I know, for instance, that Ms M would NOT see 'No More Corn!' for the compelling psychological character and moving social commentary study it is. She would probably call it melodramatic and filled with clichés.

Which is why I wasn't planning on showing it to her until *Sixteen* published it. Except I guess that's never going to happen now.

```
FtLouie:    Lilly, I don't want to burst your
            bubble, but I highly doubt we're
            going to be able to raise five grand
            from selling a teen literary maga-
            zine. I mean, our peers barely have
            time to read required stuff like O
            Pioneers!, let alone copies of some
            student-written    collection    of
            short stories and poems. I think we
            need some more feasible way to gen-
            erate cash than depending on sales
            of a magazine we haven't even writ-
            ten yet.
>
WomynRule: What do you suggest then? Candle
           selling?
```

AAAAAAHHHHHHH! Because you know in addition to the strawberry-shaped candle, there are ones shaped like bananas and pineapples. Also, birds. STATE birds. Like, for Indiana, there is a candle cardinal, the cardinal being the Hoosier state's bird.

Worse – and I hesitate to write this – there is an

actual replica of Noah's ark, with two of all the animals (even unicorns). In CANDLE form.

Even I could not make up something that revolting.

```
FtLouie:    Of course not. I just think we need
            to put a little more thought into
            the matter before we rush into—
>
SkinnerBx: Hey, Thermopolis. How's it going?
```

MICHAEL!!!! MICHAEL IS IMing ME!!!!!!!

```
FtLouie:    Sorry, Lilly, gotta go.
>
WomynRule: Why? Is my brother IMing you?
>
FtLouie:    Yeah . . .
>
WomynRule: Oh. I know what HE wants.
>
FtLouie:    Lilly, I TOLD you, we're WAITING to
            have sex—
>
WomynRule: That's not what I meant, you tool.
            I meant — Oh, never mind. Just e me
            after you've talked to him. I'm
            serious about this magazine thing,
            POG. It's the only way you're going
            to be able to see your name in
            print — besides on Us Weekly's —
            'Celebrities: They're Just Like
            Us!' pages.
>
```

```
FtLouie:    Wait — you know why Michael's IMing
            me? How do you know? What's going
            on? Tell me, Lilly—
>
WomynRule: Terminated
>
SkinnerBx: Mia? You there?
>
FtLouie:    Michael! Yes, I'm here. I'm sorry.
            I'm just having the worst day. My
            government is out of money and
            Sixteen rejected 'No More
            Corn!'!!!!!!
>
SkinnerBx: Wait — the government of Genovia is
            out of money? I didn't see anything
            about that on Netscape. How did
            THAT happen?
```

This is why my boyfriend is so wonderful. Even when he
doesn't understand a single thing that is going on in my
life, he's still, you know, way concerned for me.

```
FtLouie:    I meant the student government.
            We're in the red for five grand. And
            Sixteen rejected me.
>
SkinnerBx: Sixteen rejected 'No More Corn!'?
            How could they? That story rocks!
```

You see? You see why I love him?

```
FtLouie:    Thanks. But I guess it didn't rock
            enough for them to publish it.
>
SkinnerBx: Then they're fools. And what's this
            about being five grand in the red?
```

Briefly, I explained to Michael about the no-return recycling bins and the fact that I am going to be drawn and quartered by Amber Cheeseman as soon as she hears about her commencement taking place in Hell's Kitchen instead of Lincoln Center.

```
SkinnerBx: Come on. It can't be that bad. You
            have plenty of time to raise the
            cash.
```

Normally my boyfriend is the most astute of men. That is why he goes to an Ivy League university where he takes a course load that would prove a mental challenge even to Stephen Hawking – that genius in the wheelchair who figured out about mini black holes, as well as how to get his nurse to fall in love with him – let alone your average college student.

But sometimes . . .

Well, sometimes, he just doesn't GET it.

```
FtLouie:    Have you ever seen Amber Cheeseman,
            Michael? She may have a 4.0 and
            sound like a chipmunk when she talks,
            but she can throw a two-hundred-
            pound man over her shoulder in a
            split second, and her forearms are
            as big as Koko the gorilla's.
```

>

SkinnerBx: Hey, I know. You could try selling
candles. We did that to raise money
for the Computer Club one year!

NOOOOOOOOOOOOOOO!!!!!!!!!!! NOT YOU TOO,
MICHAEL!!!!!!!!!!

SkinnerBx: They have these candles shaped like
strawberries. Everybody in my mom
and dad's therapy groups bought
one. They smell like real strawberries.

AAAAAAAAAAAARRRRRRRRRRRGGGGGGGGG-
GGGHHHHHHHHHHH!

FtLouie: Great! Thanks for the tip!

Change the subject. NOW.

FtLouie: So how was YOUR day?

>

SkinnerBx: Not bad. We watched *THX 1138* in
class and discussed its influence on
later dystopic films from the same
era, such as *Logan's Run*, in which,
like *THX*, a young man attempts to
flee the stifling confines of the only
world he knows. Which reminds me,
what are you doing this weekend?

37

Oooh, fun! A date! Just what I need to cheer myself up.

```
FtLouie:   Going out with you.
>
SkinnerBx: That's what I was hoping you'd say.
           Only how about staying in instead
           of going out? My mom and dad are
           going out of town for a conference,
           and Maya's got to have her feet
           scraped, so they asked me if I
           could come home for the weekend to
           stay with Lilly — you know, on
           account of what happened last time
           they left her alone.
```

Do I ever. Because the last time the Drs Moscovitz let Lilly out of their sight, when they went to their country house in Albany for the weekend and allowed Lilly to stay in the apartment alone because she had a report due on Alexander Hamilton and needed Internet access, of which there is none at their country house, and Michael had finals, and the Moscovitzes' housekeeper, Maya, had to go back to the Dominican Republic to bail her nephew out of jail again, so neither of them could stay with her, Lilly invited her foot-fetishist stalker, Norman, over to interview him for a segment she was doing on *Lilly Tells It Like It Is* titled, 'Why Are Only Weirdos Attracted to Me?'

Well, Norman took umbrage at being called a weirdo, even though that's what he is. He insisted that a healthy appreciation for the foot is actually extremely sane. Then when Lilly was busy getting them Cokes in the kitchen, he snuck into her mom's room and stole her favourite pair of Manolo Blahniks!

But Lilly saw the stiletto heel sticking out of Norman's anorak pocket and made him give it back. Norman was so mad about the whole thing that he started his own website, *I Hate Lilly Moscovitz*, that has message boards and stuff that all the people who hate Lilly and her show can come and post things on (and it turns out there are a surprising number of people who hate Lilly and her TV show. Plus there are some people who don't even know who Lilly is but they joined just because they hate everything).

I have to say, after all that I'm kind of surprised the Drs Moscovitz would leave her without parental supervision, even with Michael there.

```
FtLouie:   Fun! I'll totally come over! What
           are we going to do? Watch a movie
           marathon?
```

Only, please, not a screening of one of the hideous movies he has to watch for that sci-fi film class he's taking. He's already forced me to see *Brazil*, one of the most depressing movies of all time. Can *Blade Runner*, another giant bummer of a movie, be far behind?

```
FtLouie:   Oooh, how about we watch the high-
           school seasons of Buffy on DVD? I
           just love the prom episode, when
           she gets the twinkly parasol . . .
>
SkinnerBx: Actually, I was kind of thinking of
           having a party.
```

Wait. A what? Did he say . . . PARTY?

```
FtLouie:    A party?
>
SkinnerBx: Yeah. You know. A party. An occa-
            sion on which people assemble for
            social interaction and entertain-
            ment? We can't really have parties
            here in the dorm because no one's
            room is big enough to fit more than
            like eight people. But three times
            that many can fit in my parents'
            apartment. So I figured, why not?
```

Why not? WHY NOT? Because we are not party people, Michael. We are stay-at-home-and-watch-videos people. Doesn't he remember what happened last time we had a party? Or, more accurately, the last time *I* had a party?

And I could tell he wasn't talking about Cheetos and Seven Minutes in Heaven, either. He was talking about a COLLEGE party. Everyone knows what happens at COLLEGE parties. I mean, I have seen *Animal House* (because it, along with *Caddyshack*, is one of Mr G's favourite movies of all time, and every time it's on he HAS to watch it, even if it's on one of those channels where they cut all the dirty parts out, which leaves it with practically no plot).

```
FtLouie:    I am not, under any circumstances,
            wearing a toga.
>
SkinnerBx: Not that kind of party, you goof.
```

40

                    Just a normal one, you know, with
                    music   and   food.   Next   week's
                    midterms, and everybody needs to
                    blow off a little steam beforehand.
                    And Doo Pak has never been invited
                    to a real American party before,
                    you know.

When I heard this startling fact about Michael's room-
mate, my hard, party-hating heart melted a little. Never
been invited to a real American party before! That was
just shocking! Of COURSE we had to have a party, if
only to show Doo Pak what real American hospitality is
like. Maybe I could make a vegetarian dip.

SkinnerBx: And remember Paul? Well, he's back
                    in the city, and so are Felix and
                    Trevor, so they're going to come
                    over.

My heart stopped melting. It's not that I don't like Paul,
Felix and Trevor, all members of Michael's now defunct
band. It's just that I happen to know that, while Paul,
the keyboardist, is back from Bennington where he goes
to school, because of Spring Break, Felix, the drummer,
just got out of rehab (not that there's anything wrong
with that, really, I'm glad he got help, but, um, hello,
rehab at eighteen? Scary). And Trevor, the guitar player,
is back because he got kicked out of UCLA for something so scandalous he won't even tell people what it
was.

    These are just not the kind of friends who, in my
opinion, you want to come over when your parents aren't

home. Because they might 'accidentally' set the place on fire. That's all I'm saying.

SkinnerBx: And I thought I'd invite a bunch of
          other people from the dorm.

A bunch of other people from the dorm?

My heart stopped melting even more. Because I know what that means: girls.

Because there are girls in Michael's dorm. I have seen them in the hallways when I've gone to visit him there. They wear a lot of black clothing, including berets – BERETS! – and quote lines from *The Vagina Monologues* and never read *Us Weekly*, even when they're in a doctor's office. I know because I once mentioned seeing Jessica Simpson without her make-up on in this one issue and they all just looked at me blankly. They're just like those girls from *Legally Blonde* who were very mean to Elle when she got to law school because they thought that just because she's blonde and likes clothes, she must be stupid.

I myself have encountered this kind of prejudice from these girls, since, being blonde and a princess, they just automatically assume I must be stupid. I so know what poor Princess Diana must have dealt with every single day.

I do not think I could handle being at a party with girls like this. Because girls like this know how to act at parties. They know how to smoke and drink beer.

I hate smoking. And beer smells just like that skunk that Papaw hit with the station wagon that time we were coming home from the Indiana state fair.

What is Michael *thinking*? I mean, a *party*. This is so not him.

Then again, college is a time for self-exploration and finding out who you really are and what you want to do with your life.

Oh my God! What if he's into partying now???? Partying is a very large part of the college experience. At least, according to all those movies on the Life-time Channel in which either Kellie Martin or Tiffani-Amber Thiessen star as co-eds campaigning to shut down the fraternity house at which their friend or room-mate was date raped and/or choked to death on her own vomit.

Which isn't the kind of party Michael's talking about. Right?

Wait. Michael's parents wouldn't LET him have a party like that. Even if he wanted to. Which I'm sure he doesn't. Because Michael can't stand fraternities, since he says he can't help but feel suspicious of any hetero-sexual male who would pay to belong to a club that females are not permitted to join.

Speaking of the Drs Moscovitz:

```
FtLouie:    Michael, do your parents know about
            this? This party, I mean?
>
SkinnerBx: Of course. What do you think, I'd
            do this without asking them? The
            doormen would completely rat me
            out, you know.
```

Oh. Right. The doormen. The doormen in the Moscovitzes' building know all and see all. Like Yoda.

And they babble about it like C3PO.

Still. The Drs Moscovitz are OK with this? Michael having a college party in their apartment when they aren't home . . . with *Lilly* there?

It's just so unlike them.

Wow. I totally can't believe this. Having a party with no parents around . . . that is a really big step. It's like . . . grown up.

```
SkinnerBx: So you'll come, right? The guys
           were trying to tell me there was no
           way you'd want to. On account of
           the whole princess thing.

!

FtLouie:   The princess thing? What did they
           mean by that?
>
SkinnerBx: Just, you know. I mean, it's not
           like you're much of a party girl.
```

Not much of a party girl? What does that even mean? Of course I'm not a party girl. I mean, Michael is not exactly a party guy –

At least, he didn't used to be. Before he went to college.

Oh, God. Maybe it would behove me to indicate that I am not averse to partying. Just the date rape and vomit part.

```
FtLouie:   I am TOO a party girl. I mean,
           given the right circumstances. I
```

                    mean, I like to party just as much
                    as the next girl.

I do too. This isn't even a lie. I've partied. Maybe not in
recent memory. But I'm sure I've partied. Like at my
birthday party just last year.

   And OK, it ended in disaster when my best friend got
caught making out with a busboy in the closet.

   But technically, it was still a party. Which makes me
a party girl.

   And OK, maybe not a party girl like Paris Hilton is a
party girl. I mean, I like Red Bull and all. Well, not
really, since I drank one can from my dad's mini-bar in
his suite at the Plaza and it made me stay up until four
in the morning dancing to the disco channel on digital
cable.

   But you know. Who wants to be like Paris anyway?
She can't even keep track of her dog's whereabouts half
the time. I mean, you have to find a BALANCE with the
party thing. You can't party ALL the time. Or you might
forget where you left your chihuahua. Or someone might
release an embarrassing video of you, um, partying.

   Limit the amount of partying – and Red Bull – and
you limit the amount of embarrassing videos.

   That's all I'm saying.

SkinnerBx: That's exactly what I said. Great!
           So I'll talk to you later. Love
           you. Night!
>
SkinnerBx: Terminated

Oh, God. What have I got myself into?

                            45

From the desk of
Her Royal Highness Princess Amelia Mignonette
Grimaldi Thermopolis Renaldo

Dear Dr Carl Jung,

I realize that you are still dead. However, things have suddenly got significantly worse, and I'm now convinced I will NEVER transcend my ego and achieve self-actualization.

First I find out I've bankrupted the student government and will shortly be killed by the small but extremely strong senior class valedictorian.

Then my short story gets rejected by *Sixteen* magazine.

And now my boyfriend thinks I'm going to a party he's having in his parents' apartment while they are away.

I can't really blame him for thinking this, because I sort of said I would go.

But I said I'd go because if I said no, I'd seem like a killjoy and non-party princess.

Of course, there's no way I would even be considering going if I didn't happen to remember that March is not a month where Michael is allowed to broach the subject of S-E-X to me, since last month was his allotted time to bring it up. So it's not like there can be any of THAT on his mind. You know, like during the party.

Still. I will have to socialize with people I don't know. Which I realize I do all the time in my capacity as Princess of Genovia.

But socializing with college students is quite different from socializing with other royals and dignitaries. I mean, other royals and dignitaries don't tell you all accusingly that your limo is a significant contributor to the destruction of the ozone layer, as oversized cars, such as SUVs and, yes, royal limos, cause forty-three per cent more global-warming pollution and forty-seven per cent more air pollution than an average car, the way a girl in front of Michael's dorm pointed out to me last week when I pulled up to visit him.

Could things possibly GET any worse?

I REALLY need to self-actualize. Like, right NOW. PLEASE SEND HELP.

Your friend,
Mia Thermopolis

Wednesday, March 3, Homeroom

I asked Lilly in the limo on the way to school this morning what her parents could be thinking, letting Michael have a big party in their apartment while they're away. She was like, 'Whatever. Do I look like Ruth and Morty's keeper?'

Ruth and Morty are Lilly's parents' first names. I think it is very disrespectful of her to call her own parents by their given names. *I* don't even call them by their given names, and they've asked me to about a million times.

Still, even considering how long I've known them – almost as long as Lilly has – I can only call them Dr Moscovitz. Sometimes I call them Mr Dr Moscovitz and Mrs Dr Moscovitz (but only behind their backs) when I need to specify one over the other.

But I'll never call them Ruth and Morty. Not even when Michael and I are married, and they are my in-laws. They will *always* be the Drs Moscovitz to me.

'They do realize YOU'RE going to be there, don't they?' I asked Lilly. 'I mean, at the party?'

'Duh,' Lilly said. 'Of course. What is the matter with you?'

'Nothing. I just – I'm kind of surprised that your parents are letting Michael have a party when they aren't home. It's not like them. That's all.'

'Yeah, well,' Lilly said, 'I think Ruth and Morty have bigger things to worry about.'

'Like what?'

Only I never did find out. Because right then the limo hit one of those huge potholes in front of the entrance to

48

the FDR, and Lilly and I both went sailing into the air
and hit our heads on the sunroof.

So then Lilly made me go to the nurse's office with
her when we got to school, to see if we could get notes to
get out of PE, on account of having possible concussions.

But the nurse just laughed at us.

I bet she would have given us notes if she knew they
were making us do volleyball. AGAIN. Why can't we
ever do cool sports like Pilates and yoga, like they get to
do in suburban high school?

It's so not fair.

Wednesday, March 3, US Economics

OK, so after what happened yesterday with the government money, I am fully going to start paying attention in this class now:

Scarcity – refers to the tension between our limited resources and our unlimited wants and needs.

Some examples of resources we want and need, but which are limited (scarce), include:
Goods
Services
Natural resources
Funds for the rental of gathering halls in which to conduct senior graduation

Because all resources are limited in comparison to our wants and needs, individuals as well as governments have to make decisions regarding what goods and services they can buy and which ones they must forgo.

(For instance, a government might decide that what its population really needs is recycling bins with built-in can crushers inside and the words *Paper, Cans and Battles* emblazoned across the lids.)

All individuals and governments, each having different levels of (scarce) resources, form some of their values only because they must deal with the problem of resource scarcity.

(If only Amber Cheeseman would learn to value

recycling over giving the valedictorian address at her commencement.)

So because of scarcity, people and governments must make decisions about how to allocate their resources.

(But that's what I DID!!! I made a decision over how to allocate AEHS resources – in the form of buying recycling bins – and it turned around and bit me on the butt!!!! Because I allocated incorrectly!!! WHERE IS THE PART ABOUT THIS IN THE TEXTBOOK????)

Wednesday, March 3, English

OMG, Mia! I heard about what happened at the meeting yesterday! The whole running out of money thing! I can't believe those recycle bins ended up being so expensive! And those Cans and Battles stickers! I can't figure out how that happened! I am so sorry! - Tina

> It's OK. They're replacing the *Cans and Battles* stickers. And we'll think of some way to get it. The money, I mean. Just don't tell anyone, all right? We're trying to keep it a secret until we figure out what we're going to do.

Totally! I won't tell a soul! But I had an idea. About how to raise money. Have you seen those scented candles the band was selling to raise money for their trip to Nashville?

> WE ARE NOT SELLING SCENTED CANDLES.

It was just a suggestion. I thought they were kind of nice. They have these cute little ones shaped like strawberries.

> NO CANDLES.

OK. But I know I could sell a ton to my aunts and uncles back in Saudi Arabia.

> NO CANDLES.

OK! I get it. No candles. Is there something wrong? I mean, besides the money thing? Because, no offence, but you seem . . . kinda upset. I mean, about the candles.

It's not about the candles.

What is it, then?

Nothing. Michael's parents are going out of town this weekend, and he's throwing a party in their apartment while they're gone, and he wants me to come.

But that sounds like fun!

FUN??? Are you crazy??? There are going to be COLLEGE GIRLS there.

So?

So??? What do you mean, *So???* Don't you see, Tina? If Michael sees me around a bunch of college girls at a party, he's going to realize I'm not a party girl.

But, Mia. You AREN'T a party girl.

I know that! But I don't want MICHAEL to know that!

But Michael knows you aren't a party girl. He knew you weren't a party girl when he met you. I mean, you have NEVER been a party girl. You never even

53

GO to parties. I mean, girls like Lana Weinberger, THEY go to parties, but not girls like us. We don't get INVITED to parties. We stay home Saturday nights and watch whatever is on HBO, or maybe we go out with our boyfriends, or have a sleepover with our friends. But we don't go to PARTIES. It's not like we're POPULAR.

Thanks, Tina.

Well, you know what I mean. What's wrong with not being a party girl? Why can't you just go to the party and have a good time hanging out and meeting some new people?

Because the whole idea of hanging out with a bunch of cool college girls who are going to think I'm a dorky princess makes my palms feel sweaty.

Ew. But they won't think you're a dorky princess, Mia, once they get to know you. Because you AREN'T a dorky princess.

Hello, have you MET me?

Well, OK. You're a princess. But you're not a dork. I mean, you're practically failing Geometry. How dorky is that?

But that's exactly what I mean! These girls are SMART, they got into an Ivy League university, and I'm . . . practically failing Geometry.

If you really don't want to go, why don't you tell Michael you have to do something with your grandmother that night?

I can't! Michael was so excited when I said yes!!!! I don't want to break his heart AGAIN. I mean, it's bad enough I have to do it every three months when he asks me whether I've changed my mind about the whole sex thing (like there's really a chance I'm going to. And OK, he's a guy, so it's not like he's ever seen Kirsten Dunst's heart-wrenching portrayal of an unwed teen mom in *Fifteen and Pregnant* on the Lifetime Channel).

But still. I am ONLY FIFTEEN. I'm not ready to give up the golden bough of my virginity!

Not until your Senior Prom, anyway! On a king-sized feather bed at the Four Seasons!

Totally. And, while I know Michael is the most faithful and steadfast of lovers, if I don't go to the party, the lure of an exotic college girl, dancing suggestively on his parents' coffee table, might be too much even for HIM to resist! Do you see my difficulty now?

Hey, you guys. Guess what?

Oh! Hi, Lilly!

Um. Hi, Lilly.

What were you guys just talking about?

Nothing.

Nothing.

Yeah, you so clearly were NOT talking about nothing. But whatever. I think I may have the solution to our financial problems. Guess who said she'd be the advisor for our new literary magazine?

Lilly, I totally appreciate your enthusiasm about this, but a literary magazine isn't going to generate enough income to make up for what we've already lost. In fact, with printing costs and all, it's just going to cause us to have to spend MORE money we don't have.

A literary magazine? That sounds like so much fun! And then you'll have a place to publish 'No More Corn!', Mia!

I can't let 'No More Corn!' be printed in a school literary magazine.

Oh, I suppose your story is too good to be in a mere student-published periodical.

That's not it at all. I just don't want the Guy Who Hates It When They Put Corn In The Chilli to read it. I mean, come on. He KILLS himself at the end.

Oh! That WOULD be awkward! I mean, if he

realized the story is about him. It might hurt his feelings.

Exactly.

Funny how this didn't worry you when you were trying to get your story published in *Sixteen*, a national magazine with a million readers.

No self-respecting boy would be caught dead reading *Sixteen* magazine, and you know it, Lilly. But he's totally likely to read a school-run literary magazine!

Whatever. Look, Ms Martinez loves the idea of a school lit mag. I asked her just before class, and she said she thought it was great, since Albert Einstein High School has a newspaper but not a literary magazine, and it will be a great opportunity for the student population's many artists, poets and storytellers to see their craft in print.

Um, yeah, but unless we're going to CHARGE them to publish their stuff, I don't see how that's going to raise US any cash.

Don't you see, Mia? We can charge people for copies of the magazine once we've printed it. I bet we'll sell LOTS of copies!

Thank you, Tina. The lack of jadedness in your response is quite refreshing compared to SOME people's negative attitudes.

I'm sorry. I'm really not trying to be negative. I'm just trying to be practical. We'd be better off selling candles.

Oooooh, you should see the cute Noah's Ark candles they have! They've got all the animals, two by two . . . even tiny little unicorns! Are you SURE you don't want to consider candle selling, Mia?

AAAAAARRRRRRGGGGGGGHHHHHH!!!!

Oh, sorry. I guess not.

Wednesday, March 3, French

I heard about what's going on. – Shameeka

WHO TOLD YOU????

Ling Su. She feels awful about it. She doesn't know how she messed up like that.

Oh, the money thing. Well, it's not really her fault. And listen, we're kind of trying to keep it a secret. So could you not mention it to anyone?

I totally understand. I mean, when the seniors find out, they are NOT going to be happy. Especially Amber Cheeseman. She may look small, but I hear she's strong as an ape.

Yeah, that's what I mean. That's why we're trying to keep it on the low down.

Gotcha. My lips are sealed.

Thanks, Shameeka.

Hey, you guys. Is it true? - Perin

Is WHAT true?

About the student government being broke.

WHO TOLD YOU?

Um, I heard it from the receptionist this morning in

59

the attendance office when I brought in my late pass. But don't worry, I won't tell. She said not to.

Oh. Well. Yes. It's true.

And you're starting a literary magazine to make up for the lost revenue?

Who told you that?

Lilly. Can I just say that, even though I think starting a literary magazine is a neat idea and all, when we needed to make some money fast at my old school, we sold the cutest scented candles in the shapes of actual fruits and we made a mint!

What a great idea! Don't you think so, Mia?

NO!

Wednesday, March 3, Gifted and Talented

So at lunch today Boris Pelkowski put his tray down next to mine and said, 'So I hear we're broke.'

And I seriously lost it.

'YOU GUYS,' I yelled at the entire lunch table. 'YOU HAVE TO STOP TALKING ABOUT THIS. WE'RE TRYING TO KEEP IT A SECRET.'

Then I explained about how much I value my life and how I do not care for it to be cut short by an enraged hapkido brown-belt valedictorian with monkey-like strength in her upper torso (even if, by killing and/or maiming me, she would actually be doing me a favour, since then I wouldn't have to live with the humiliation of having my boyfriend forsake me because I am not a party girl).

'She would never kill you, Mia,' Boris pointed out helpfully. 'Lars would shoot her first.'

Lars, who was showing Tina's bodyguard, Wahim, all the games on his new Sidekick, looked up upon hearing his name.

'Who is planning to kill the princess?' Lars asked alertly.

'No one,' I said from between gritted teeth. 'Because we're going to get the money before she ever finds out. RIGHT????'

I think I must have really impressed them with my seriousness, since they all went, 'OK.'

Then Perin thankfully changed the subject.

'Uh-oh, looks like they did it again,' she said, pointing to the Guy Who Hates It When They Put Corn In The Chilli. Because he was sitting in his usual place, by himself, disgustedly picking pieces of corn from his bowl of chilli, and flicking them on to his lunch tray.

'That poor guy,' Perin said with a sigh. 'I feel so bad whenever I see him sitting alone like that. I know how that feels.'

There was a painful pause as we all recalled how Perin had sat by herself at the beginning of the school year because she was new. Until we adopted her, that is.

'I thought he got a girlfriend,' Tina said. 'Didn't you say you saw him buying prom tickets last year, Mia?'

'Yes,' I replied with a sigh. 'But I was wrong. It turned out he was only asking the people who were selling the prom tickets if they knew where the closest F-train station was.'

Which, incidentally, is what inspired my short story about him.

'It's so sad,' Tina said, gazing in the direction of the Guy Who Hates It When They Put Corn In The Chilli. 'It makes me think that what happens in Mia's short story about him could happen in real life.'

!!!!!

'Maybe we should ask him to sit with us,' I said. Because the last thing I need, on top of everything else, is the guilt of having caused some guy to commit suicide by not being nicer to him.

'No, thank you,' Boris said. 'I have enough problems digesting this disgusting food without having to do so in the company of a bona-fide weirdo.'

'Hello,' Lilly said under her breath. 'Pot, this is kettle. You're black.'

'I heard that,' Boris said, looking pained.

'You were meant to,' Lilly sang.

Then Lilly pulled a bunch of flyers from her Hello

Kitty Trapper Keeper. She'd clearly been down in the office, photocopying something. She started passing the photocopies around.

'Everybody give these out in your afternoon classes,' she said. 'Hopefully by tomorrow we'll get enough submissions to run our first issue by the end of this week.'

I looked down at the bright pink flyer. It said:

HEY YOU!

Are you sick and tired of being told what's hot and what's not by the so-called media?

Do you want to read stories written by your peers, about issues that really matter to you, instead of the stream of pap we are fed by teen magazines and our parents' newspapers?

Then submit your original articles, poetry, short stories, cartoons, manga, novellas, and photos to Albert Einstein High School's First Ever Literary Magazine

FAT LOUIE'S PINK BUTTHOLE!!!!

Fat Louie's Pink Butthole now accepting submissions for Volume 1, Issue 1

Oh my God.

OH MY GOD.

'Before you go all reactionary about the name of our literary magazine, Mia,' Lilly began – I guess because she must have noticed my lips turning white – 'may I just point out that it is extremely creative and that, if we stick with it, we will never have to worry about any other literary magazine in the world having the same name.'

'Because it's named after my cat's butt!'

'Yes,' Lilly said. 'It is. Thanks to the movies based on your life, your cat is famous, Mia. Everyone knows who Fat Louie is. That is why our magazine is going to sell. Because when people realize it has something to do with the Princess of Genovia, they will snatch it right up. Because, for reasons that are beyond me, people are actually interested in you.'

'But the title isn't about ME!' I wailed. 'It's about my cat! My cat's butt, to be exact!'

'Yes,' Lilly said. 'I will admit it's a bit on the juvenile side. But that is why it will get people's attention. They won't be able to look away. I figure for the first cover, I'll take a picture of Fat Louie's butt, and then—'

She kept on talking, but I wasn't listening. I COULDN'T listen.

Why must I be surrounded by so many lunatics?

Wednesday, March 3, Earth Science

Kenny just asked me to rewrite our worksheet on sub-duction zones. Not do the actual WORK over again (although it wouldn't really be over again, since I didn't do it in the first place. He did), but to redo it on a new sheet that isn't covered in pizza stains like the one we would be handing in if I wasn't redoing it, due to the fact that Kenny did it last night while he was eating his dinner.

I wish Kenny would be more careful with our home-work. It's a big pain for me to have to copy it over. Lilly's not the only one with carpal, you know. I mean, SHE isn't the one who has to sign a gazillion autographs for people every time she gets out of her limo in front of the Plaza. People have started LINING UP there every day after school, because they know I'll be coming for my princess lesson with Grandmere. I have to keep a Sharpie with me at all times just for that reason.

Writing *Princess Mia Thermopolis* over and over again is no joke. I wish my name weren't so long.

Maybe I should just switch to writing *HRH Mia*. But would that seem stuck-up?

Kenny just showed me the *Fat Louie's Pink Butthole* flyer and asked if I thought his thesis on brown dwarf stars would be suitable for publication.

'I don't know,' I told him. 'I have nothing to do with it.'

'But it's named after your cat,' he said, looking dis-mayed.

'Yeah,' I said. 'But I still have nothing to do with it.'

He doesn't seem to believe me.

I can't say I blame him.

Homework:

Homeroom: N/A
PE: WASH GYM SHORTS!!!
US Economics: Chapter 8
English: pages 116–132, *O Pioneers!*
French: *écrivez une histoire comique pour vendredi*
G and T: figure out what I'm going to wear to The Party
Geometry: worksheet
Earth Science: ask Kenny

Don't forget: Tomorrow is Grandmere's birthday! Bring gift to school so I can give it to her at Princess Lessons!!!!!!!!

Wednesday, March 3, the Plaza Hotel

Something is definitely up with Grandmere. I knew this the minute I walked into her suite, because she was being WAY too nice to me. She was like, 'Amelia! How lovely to see you! Sit down! Have a bonbon!' and shoved all these truffles from La Maison du Chocolat in my face.

Oh yeah. Something's going on.

Either that or she's drunk. Again.

AEHS should really do a convocation about coping with alcoholic grandparents. Because I could use some tips.

'Good news,' she announced. 'I think I might be able to help you with your little financial predicament.'

WHOA. WHOA!!!!!! Grandmere is coming through with a loan? Oh, thank you, God! THANK YOU!

'When I was in school,' she went on, 'and we ran low on funds for our spring trip to Paris to visit the couture houses one year, we put on a show.'

I nearly choked on my tea. 'You WHAT?'

'Put on a show,' Grandmere said. 'It was *The Mikado*, you know. That we put on, I mean. Gilbert and Sullivan. Quite difficult, particularly since we were an all-girls school, and there are so many male leads. I remember Genevieve – you know, the one who used to dip my braids into her inkwell when I wasn't looking – was just sick over having to play the Mikado.' An evil grin spread across Grandmere's face. 'The Mikado was supposed to be quite large, you know. I suppose Genevieve was upset about being typecast.'

OK. So obviously no loan was forthcoming. Grandmere just felt like taking a little jog down memory lane and had decided to drag me along with her.

I wondered if she'd even notice if I started text-messaging Michael. He'd just be getting out of his Stochastic Analysis and Optimization class.

'I had the starring role, of course,' Grandmere was going on, lost in reverie. 'The ingénue, Yum-Yum. People said I was the finest Yum-Yum they had ever seen, but I'm sure they were only trying to flatter me. Still, with my twenty-inch waist I did look absurdly fetching in a kimono.'

Text message: STUCK W/GM

'No one was more surprised than I was when it turned out there was a Broadway director in the audience – Señor Eduardo Fuentes, one of the most influential stage directors of his day – and he approached me after opening night with an offer to star in the show he was directing in New York. I never even considered it, of course –'

Text message: I MISS U

'– since I knew I was destined for much greater things than a career in the theatre. I wanted to be a surgeon, or perhaps a fashion designer, like Coco Chanel.'

Text message: I LUV U

'He was devastated, of course. I wouldn't be surprised if it turned out he was a little bit in love with me. I did look smart in that kimono. But of course, my parents never would have approved. And if I HAD gone to New York with him, I'd never have met your grandfather.'

Text message: GET ME OUT OF HERE

'You should have heard my rendition of "Three Little Maids":
    "Three little maids from school are we –"'

Text message: OMG SHE IS SINGING SEND
HELP NOW

'"Pert as a schoolgirl well can be –"'
    Fortunately Grandmere broke off at that point in a coughing fit. 'Oh, dear! Yes. I was quite the sensation that year, let me tell you.'

Text message: THIS IS WORSE THAN WHAT
AC WILL DO 2 ME WHEN SHE FINDS OUT
ABOUT THE $

'Amelia, what are you doing with that mobile phone?'
    'Nothing,' I said, quickly pressing Send.
    Grandmere's face still had a dewy look from her stroll down memory lane.
    'Amelia. I have an idea.'
    Oh, no.
    See, there are two people in my acquaintance from whom you never want to hear the words, 'I have an idea.'
    Lilly is one.
    Grandmere is the other.
    'Would you look at that?' I pointed at the clock. 'Six o'clock already. Well, I better get going, I'm sure you

have dinner plans with some shah or something. Isn't it your birthday tomorrow? You must have some pre-birthday reflection to do . . .'

'Sit back down, Amelia,' Grandmere said in her scariest voice.

I sat.

'I think,' Grandmere said, 'that you should put on a show.'

At least, that's what I could have sworn she said.

But that couldn't be correct. Because no one in her right mind would say something like that.

Wait. Did I just write 'in her right mind'?

'A show?' I knew Grandmere had recently cut back on her smoking. She hadn't quit or anything. But her doctor told her if she didn't cut back she'd be on an oxygen tank by the time she's seventy.

So Grandmere had started limiting her cigarettes to after meals only. This is on account of her not being able to find an oxygen tank that goes with any of her designer outfits.

I decided maybe the nicotine patch she was wearing had backfired or something, sending pure, unadulterated carbon monoxide into her bloodstream.

Because that was the only explanation I could think of for why she might possibly consider it a good idea for Albert Einstein High School to put on a show.

'Grandmere,' I said. 'Maybe you should peel off your patch. Slowly. And I'll just call your doctor—'

'Don't be ridiculous, Amelia,' she said, sniffing at the suggestion that she might be suffering from any sort of brain aneurysm or stroke, either of which, at her age, are highly likely, according to Yahoo! Health. 'It is a perfectly reasonable idea for a fundraiser. People have been

70

putting on benefits and amateur entertainments for centuries to generate donations for their cause.'

'But, Grandmere,' I said. 'The Drama Club is already putting on a show this spring, the musical *Hair*. They've started rehearsals and everything.'

'So? A little competition might make things more interesting for them,' Grandmere said.

'Uh,' I said. How was I going to break it to Grandmere that her idea was totally sub par? Like, almost as bad as selling candles. Or starting a literary magazine and calling it *Fat Louie's Pink Butthole*?

'Grandmere,' I said. 'I appreciate your concern for my economic blunder. But I do not need your help. OK? Really, it's going to be all right. I will find a way to raise the cash myself. Lilly and I are already on it, and we—'

'Then you may tell Lilly,' Grandmere said, 'that your financial problems are over, since it is your grand-mother's intention to put on a play that will have the theatre community begging for tickets, and everyone who is anyone in New York society dying to be involved. It will be a completely original spectacle in order to showcase your myriad talents.'

She must have meant Lilly's talents. Because I have no theatrical skills.

'Grandmere,' I said. 'No. I really mean it. We don't need your help. We're fine, OK? Just fine. Whatever you're thinking of doing, cut it out. Because I swear, if you butt in again, I'll call Dad. Don't think I won't!'

But Grandmere had already drifted away, asking her maid to find her Rolodex . . . she apparently had some calls to make.

Well, it shouldn't be too hard to stop her. I can just tell Principal Gupta not to let her into the building.

71

With the new security cameras and all, they can't claim they didn't see her coming: she doesn't go anywhere without a stretch limo and a hairless miniature poodle. She can't be too hard to spot.

Wednesday, March 3, the Loft

Lilly says Grandmere must be projecting her feelings of powerlessness over being outbid by John Paul Reynolds-Abernathy the Third for the fake island of Genovia on to my problems with the student government's financial situation.

'It's a classic case of transference,' is what Lilly said when I called her a little while ago to beg her one last time to change the name of her literary magazine. 'I don't understand why you're so upset about it. If it makes her happy, why not let her put on her little play? I'll happily play the lead . . . I have no problem taking on yet another responsibility, in addition to the vice-presidency, my role as creator, director and star of *Lilly Tells It Like It Is*, and editing *Fat Louie's Pink Butthole*.'

'Yeah,' I said. 'About that, Lilly . . .'

'Well, it was my idea, wasn't it?' Lilly reminded me. 'Shouldn't I be editor? This magazine's going to ROCK, we've had so many kickass contributions already.'

'Lilly,' I said, mustering all my carefully honed leadership qualities and speaking in a calm, measured voice, the way my dad addresses Parliament. 'I don't care about your being editor and all that. And I think it's great and everything that you're doing this – providing a forum in which the artists and writers of AEHS can express themselves. But don't you think we need to concentrate on how we're going to raise the five grand we need for the seniors' gradua—'

'*Fat Louie's Pink Butthole* IS going to raise five grand,' Lilly said confidently. 'It's going to raise MORE than five grand. It's going to raise the roof off the publishing industry as we know it. *Sixteen* magazine is going to be put out of business when people get hold of *Fat Louie's Pink Butthole* and read the honest, raw pieces it contains, slices of American teen life that will have *Sixty Minutes* pounding on my door, demanding interviews, and no doubt Quentin Tarantino, asking for the film rights—'

'Wow,' I said, barely listening. Am I the ONLY person who recognizes the GREAT pain we are going to be in when Amber Cheeseman finds out we have no money to pay for Alice Tully Hall? 'The contributions you've got are that good, huh?'

'Spectacular. I had no idea our fellow students were so DEEP. Kenny Showalter in particular wrote an ode to his true love that brought tears to my—'

'Kenny wrote an ode?'

'Well, he CALLS it a thesis about brown dwarf stars, but it is clearly a tribute to a woman. A woman he once loved, then tragically lost.'

Whoa. Who had KENNY ever loved and lost? Except . . .

Me?

But I couldn't let this news distract me! It was important to stay on point. I HAD to get Lilly to change the name of her literary magazine.

Oh, and make five thousand dollars –

Ooooh! Michael's IMing me!

```
SkinnerBx: Hey! So what was the deal with your
           grandmother? Was she really singing?
>

FtLouie:   What? Oh, yeah! Among other things.
           How are you?
>
```

```
SkinnerBx: Great.  Still stoked you're coming
           over this weekend.
```

OK, my life is so seriously over. I thought Amber Cheeseman was going to be the death of me, but it turns out I'm going to die well before she ever finds out I've squandered her commencement money on environmentally friendly recycling bins: I am going to have to kill MYSELF first, because that's the only way I can see to get out of going to this party.

Because I CAN'T go to this party. I CAN'T. See, I know what's going to happen if I go: I'm going to be all shy and intimidated by the much smarter, older people there, and I'm going to end up sitting by myself in a corner, and Michael is going to come over and be like, 'Is everything OK?' and I'm going to be like, 'Yes,' but he will know I am lying because my nostrils will flare (note to self: does he know about how my nostrils flare when I lie??? Find out) and then he'll figure out I'm not a party girl and am, in fact, the total social drag I know myself to be.

Besides, I don't even own a beret.

I'm not going to let this happen. Because I'm just going to say I can't go.

OK. Here I go.

```
FtLouie:   Michael, I'm really sorry, but—
```

DELETE DELETE DELETE

I CAN'T say No. Because what if he takes it personally? What if he thinks it's like a rejection of HIM?
WHAT IF HE SEEKS SOLACE FOR HIS INJURED

PRIDE IN THE ARMS OF ONE OF THOSE MEAN COLLEGE GIRLS????

Wait. I've got to pull myself together. Michael isn't like that. He would never cheat on me with another girl, no matter how hard she threw herself at him. Even if Craig DID cheat on Ashley with Manny on *Degrassi* when Ashley wouldn't have sex with him. That doesn't mean Michael would do the same thing. Because he is BETTER than Craig. Who by the way was suffering from bipolar disorder at the time. And is also a fictional character.

Besides, college girls don't wear thongs. They think they are sexist.

Tina is right. I've just got to be honest with him. I've got to come out and say it:

```
FtLouie:   Michael, I can't go to your party
           because I don't even like parties
           and besides I think it's going to
           be totally boring hanging out with
           a bunch of college people, espe-
           cially if you all talk about
           dystopic sci-fi films . . .
```

DELETE DELETE DELETE

I can't say THAT! Oh God. What am I going to do????

```
FtLouie:   Yeah! Can't wait!
```

God. I am such a liar.

```
SkinnerBx: So what's this I hear about your
           grandmother having some kind of
           party next Wednesday night for Bob
           Dylan?
>
FtLouie:   Bob Dylan? You mean the singer?
>
SkinnerBx: Yeah. Bono and Elton John are sup-
           posed to be there too.
```

For a minute I thought maybe Michael had inhaled too much second-hand marijuana smoke from the dorm room across the hall from his.

Then I remembered Grandmere's benefit to raise money for the Genovian olive farmers.

```
FtLouie:   Oh, right. Wow, that's funny. How
           did you hear about that?
>
SkinnerBx: Netscape. Apparently she's hosting
           something called Aide de Ferme?
```

Farm Aid. I should have known.

```
FtLouie:   Oh. Yeah. She is.
>
SkinnerBx: So is there a chance you can sneak
           me in? I'd love to ask Bob if he
           still believes an individual can
           change the world as we know it with
           a single song. Do you think that
           would be OK? I promise not to
```

> embarrass you in front of any world
> leaders.

Oh! How sweet! Michael wants to meet a celebrity! That is so not like him.

But then, Bob Dylan isn't your average celebrity. After all, he practically invented his own language. At least, that's what it sounds like, whenever Michael puts on one of his CDs.

Still, Michael will no doubt find a use for Bob's sage, Yoda-like musical wisdom. He seems to have no problem figuring out what Bob is saying.

And, as an added plus for me, I get a date for next Wednesday night!

And OK, he's basically just using me to meet Bob Dylan. But whatever.

See, that's the great thing about having a boyfriend. When you've had the suckiest day imaginable, all he has to do is ask you out, and it's like: poof! Bad stuff begone. Really, it's some powerful stuff, the whole boyfriend thing.

FtLouie: That sounds like it should be
         doable.

Michael then went on to write very nice things to me, like what an effective leader I am, both of Genovia and AEHS, and how much he can't wait to see me this weekend, and what he's going to do to me when he DOES see me, and how he thinks I'm the best writer in the world, and how Shonda Yost, *Sixteen* magazine's fiction editor, must have been on crack not to pick 'No More Corn!' as the winner of her contest.

Which was all very nice, but didn't really do anything to address the problem that was REALLY weighing on my mind:

What am I going to do about his party?

Oh, yeah. And how am I going to get the money to rent Alice Tully Hall?

Thursday, March 4, the Limo on the way to school

I'm so tired. Last night just as I was getting into bed, I got an IM. I thought it must be Michael, writing to say he loved me. You know, one last time before he went to sleep.

But it was BORIS PELKOWSKI, of all people.

JoshBell2: Mia! What's this I hear about your grandmother having a party next Wednesday night and inviting celebrated violinist and my personal artistic hero, Joshua Bell, to it?

Good grief.

FtLouie: Joshua Bell wouldn't happen to be considering buying an island in The World off the coast of Dubai, would he?

>

JoshBell2: I don't know about that. He could be buying Indiana, the great state from which he hails, and which happens to be the birthplace of many other musical geniuses as well, including Hoagy Carmichael and Michael Jackson. If it wouldn't be too much trouble, Mia — could you get me into that party? I have GOT to meet him. There's something very important I have to tell Joshua Bell.

80

You know, Boris might be hot now. But he's still weird.

```
FtLouie:   I can probably figure out a way to
           sneak you in.
>
JoshBell2: Oh THANK YOU, Mia! You don't know
           how much I appreciate it. If
           there's anything I can ever do for
           you — besides rehearse in the sup-
           ply closet, which I already do —
           let me know!
```

As if that weren't random enough, then Ling Su IMed me.

```
Painturgrl:Hey, Mia! I heard your grandma is
           having a party on Wednesday night,
           and Matthew Barney, the controver-
           sial conceptual artist, is going to
           be there.
>
FtLouie:   Let me guess: Matthew Barney is
           buying an island in The World off
           the coast of Dubai.
>
Painturgrl:How did you guess? He's buying
           Iceland for his wife, Björk. Any
           chance you could smuggle me in to
           meet him?
>
FtLouie:   No problem.
>
Painturgrl:Mia Thermopolis, you rule!
```

Then came one from Shameeka:

```
Beyonce_Is_Me:  Hi, Mia!
>
FtLouie:        Wait, I already know: You
                heard Beyonce is coming to the
                party my grandmother is giv-
                ing Wednesday night to raise
                money for the Genovian olive
                farmers, and you'd like me to
                sneak you in so you can meet
                her.
>
Beyonce_Is_Me:  Actually, it's Halle Berry.
                She's buying California. Is
                BEYONCÉ going to be there
                too????
>
FtLouie:        Consider yourself invited.
>
Beyonce_Is_Me:  REALLY???? YOU ARE THE BEST!!!
```

Then Kenny:

```
E=mc²:    Mia, is it true your grandmother is
          hosting a party next week at which
          the world-renowned scientist Dr
          Rita Coldwell will be in atten-
          dance?
>
FtLouie:  Probably. Want to come?
>
E=mc²:    COULD I? Thanks so much, Mia!
```

```
>
FtLouie:   Don't mention it.
```

Then Tina:

```
Iluvromance:  Mia, is it true your grandmother
              is having a party and all these
              celebrities  are  going  to  be
              there?
>
FtLouie:      Yes. Which one do you want to
              meet?
>
Iluvromance:  I don't care! ANY celebrity is
              fine with me!
>
FtLouie:      Done. Be there or be square.
>
Iluvromance:  EEEEEEEEEEEEEEEEEEEEEEEE!!!
              CELEBRITIES!!! I'M SO EXCITED!!!
```

Then, finally, Lilly:

```
WomynRule: Hey! What's this I hear about your
           grandma  inviting  Madonna  to  some
           party next Wednesday night?
```

Whoa. Not Madonnar too. What's she bidding on?
Faux Malawi?

```
FtLouie:   You want to come and meet her?
>
WomynRule: You know I do. She and I have a few
```

```
            things I need to discuss. Primarily
            her support of the Taliban for all
            those years.
>
FtLouie:    Be my guest.
>
WomynRule:  Rockin'. See ya tomorrow, POG.
```

I guess all that stuff I wrote to Carl Jung about – you
know, being the president of my student government,
but still super unpopular – turns out not to be true. I'm
QUITE popular.

Thanks to my GRANDMA.

Thursday, March 4, Homeroom

I'm going to kill her.

I told her NO. I specifically and definitively said NO to her.

How can she do this to me?

Again?

Thursday, March 4, PE

Seriously. How did she even DO it? I mean, so fast?

And they're everywhere, of course. The walls are plastered with them. I opened my locker and one popped out into my hand.

SHE STUFFED THEM INTO EVERYONE'S LOCKER.

That had to have taken HOURS. How did she do it? Who did she PAY to do it?

God. It could have been anyone. A teacher, even. They barely earn a living wage, after all. I know, I've seen Mr G's pay stubs lying around.

Everyone is walking around with one in their hand. A bright yellow flyer that says:

AUDITIONS TODAY, 3:30 P.M.
The Plaza Hotel, Grand Ballroom
A brand-new, all-original show

Braid!

All Are Welcome
No Theatrical Experience Necessary

I already overheard some of the Drama Club members – the ones who have been busy rehearsing for *Hair* – looking around all darkly under their eyebrow piercings and going, '*Braid!?* What's *Braid!?* I never heard of a show called *Braid!*. Is it a new Andrew Lloyd Webber? Is it about Rapunzel?'

They are furious that someone is putting on a theatrical production – especially one that seems to involve hair – that might draw away THEIR audience.

And I can't say I blame them.

But I am not about to volunteer the information that my GRANDMOTHER is the someone they're all looking for. I mean, Amber Cheeseman is not the only person in this school who knows how to kill with a single blow of the heel of her hand. Some of those drama people. . . they know how to use swords and stuff. Like in FENCING.

I do NOT need any rapiers to my heart, thanks very much.

Don't even get me started on nunchucks.

What can Grandmere be *thinking*? What is *Braid!*?

And why can't she ever just stay OUT OF MY LIFE??? It's not like I don't have ENOUGH problems, thank you very much. I mean, just this morning, when I went into Rocky's bedroom to kiss him goodbye before I left for school, he pointed at me all happily and shrieked, 'Tuck!'

Yes. My brother thinks I'm a truck.

WHY AM I THE ONLY ONE WHO SEES THAT THIS MIGHT BE A POTENTIAL PROBLEM????

Thursday, March 4, US Economics

OK, so paying attention now:

The focus of economics is to understand the problem of scarcity. How do we fulfil the unlimited wants of humankind with the limited and/or scarce resources available?

This is called utility – the advantage or fulfilment a person receives from consuming goods or a service.

The more the person or government consumes, the larger the total utility will be.

So Grandmere's utility must be the biggest in the WHOLE ENTIRE WORLD.

Oh my God. Lana knows.

I don't know how she found out, but she knows. I know she knows because she came up to me in the hallway and went, 'I know.'

!!!!!!!!!!!!!!

And she said it all *knowingly*. You know?

The thing is . . . I don't know WHAT she knows. Does she know Grandmere is the one behind the rival show?

Or does she know about how I blew all the seniors' money?

Or does she know about – gasp! – my fear that Michael is going to find out I'm not a party girl?

But how COULD she? I have confided this fear to no one – no one except Tina Hakim Baba, and telling her a secret is like telling it to a wall. She'd NEVER tell.

Especially not LANA.

Still, whatever it is, Lana knows, she says she won't tell . . .

. . . But only if I meet her demands.

HER DEMANDS!!!

She says to meet her in the third-floor stairwell right after lunch, where she'll tell me what she wants to maintain her silence.

I didn't know the popular people knew about the third-floor stairwell. I thought that was the sole reserve of the geeks.

God, I wonder what she wants. What if she, like, wants to be my best friend?

Seriously! Like what if she wants me to pretend to like her so she gets HER picture in *Us Weekly* alongside mine? Or so she can come along to the next royal wedding I attend, and schmooze with Prince William? You so know she's just WAITING for a chance to get him alone so she can show him why her name is the one most often scrawled on the stall doors of the AEHS men's rooms (according to Boris).

But wait . . . what if that's not it at all? What if she doesn't want me to pretend to be her friend, but instead she wants my resignation as president – so SHE can be president????

It's totally possible. I mean, she never really DID get over my beating her in the election. I mean, she PRE-TENDED not to care – telling everyone, after she lost, that being student-body president is stupid anyway, and that she didn't know what she was thinking, ever running for the post in the first place.

But what if she's changed her mind? What if she doesn't REALLY think it's stupid after all, and wants my job?

Although would that necessarily be the worst thing? I mean, being president is a lot of work for basically noth-ing. I haven't got even a single thank-you for the recy-cling bins.

And I know the signs on them are spelled wrong, but still.

Although if Lana demands my resignation, at least it will free up a bunch of my schedule. I mean, then maybe I'd have time to work on that book I've been meaning to start writing. I could expand 'No More Corn!' into a novel. I could try to sell it to an actual publisher. I wouldn't have to worry about the Guy Who Hates It When They Put Corn In The Chilli reading it either, because what high-school kid has time to read books for pleasure? None.

And then I could be published, and go on Book TV and talk all knowledgeably about symbolism and stuff.

God. That would be so great.

But wait. Lana CAN'T take over being president, even if I resign. If I resign, Lilly, as VP, will get the job.

So that CAN'T be what Lana wants. She must want something else from me.

But what? I have NOTHING. She's got to know that. Nothing except the throne of Genovia awaiting me at some date in the future . . .

Could THAT be what she wants? Not my throne, but like, my CROWN?

I can't give my tiara away. My dad would kill me. It's worth like a million bucks or something. That's why Grandmere has to keep it in the vault at the Plaza.

WAIT – WHAT IF SHE WANTS MICHAEL???

But why would she? She never wanted him when he was here at AEHS. In fact, for some reason, she seemed to find him completely dorky and unappealing (has anyone ever BEEN as blind?).

Besides, I heard that lately she's been dating the Dalton basketball team.

She'd BETTER not want Michael, that's all I can say. I mean, she can have my throne.

BUT NEVER MY BOYFRIEND.

Mia, what's wrong? – T

Nothing's wrong! What makes you think something's wrong?

Because you look like you just swallowed a sock.

91

Do I? I don't mean to. Nothing's wrong. Nothing at all.

Oh. I thought something might have happened with Michael. Did you talk to him yet? About your not being a party girl, I mean?

Um. No.

Mia! You have to be firm with guys. It's like Ms Dynamite says in 'Put Him Out' - I understand you love him and ur down/But that don't mean you gotta b his clown.

I KNOW!

You guys. We have SO MANY submissions for the first issue. Ms Martinez and I are meeting at lunch to decide what's going in and what's not. Issue 1 of *Fat Louie's Pink Butthole* is going to ROCK.

PLEASE STOP CALLING IT THAT.

No, because that's its NAME. You're the only one who doesn't like it. Well, except Principal Gupta. But like HER opinion counts. Speaking of which, POG, what's this *Braid!* thing your grandmother's got going on?

How do you know it's her????

Um, who else would hold auditions at the *Plaza*? Duh. So. What is it?

I don't know. Just another of my crazy grandmother's schemes to humiliate and annoy me.

God, who peed in YOUR cornflakes this morning?

NO ONE!!! I'm just sick of her always butting into my life!!!

Mia's worried about Michael finding out she's not a party girl.

TINA!!!!!!!!!!!

Well, I'm sorry, Mia. But it's so ridiculous. Don't you think it's ridiculous, Lilly?

What's a party girl?

You know. Like Lana. Or Paris Hilton.

UGH!!!! Why would you want to be like Paris Hilton, any-way????

I don't. That's not what I'm worried about.
I'm just—

Paris Hilton is one of those women who is too pretty to live. Don't you think, Tina?

Totally. She is NO ONE for you to be threatened by, Mia.

I am not threatened by her! I just—

93

Check it out:

WOMEN WHO ARE TOO BEAUTIFUL TO LIVE AND SHOULD BE SENT AWAY TO LIVE WITH ONE ANOTHER ON A DESERTED ISLAND SO THE REST OF US CAN STOP FEELING SO INADEQUATE
By
Lilly Moscovitz

1) Paris Hilton: Wait — she's pretty, can eat whatever she wants and never get fat, much less have to exercise, AND she's an heiress? Is there no JUSTICE on this planet? And OK, she is kind to animals and gay people, and she is obviously smart enough to have landed herself a fiancé who is related to one of the richest families in the world. But did she ever think about using her mind to develop something other than a reality TV show? What about a cure for cancer, Paris? What about a way to atomize sea-water to produce droplets to rise into the clouds and increase their reflectivity of sunlight, resulting in cooling temperatures adequate to compensate for global warming, thus saving the planet? Come on, Paris, we know you could do it if you applied yourself. With your money and brains, you could really make a difference!

2) Angelina Jolie: Just get rid of her! She's way too beautiful, with those stupid pouty lips and all that hair and those sticky-outy hip bones. I don't care about any of that stealing Brad from Jennifer stuff, or the Ethiopian orphan she adopted, or whether or not she ever made out with her brother. Just get rid of her! She's too pretty!

3) Keira Knightley: Oh my God, I HATE her! She's WAY too beauti-

94

ful to live! It's bad enough she got to make out with Orlando in *Pirates*, but now she also plays Elizabeth Bennett in yet another *Pride and Prejudice* remake? I am sorry, but she's no Lizzie Bennett. Lizzie Bennett is supposed to be SMART, not beautiful. That's the whole point of the story — that Lizzie isn't traditionally gorgeous the way Keira is. GOD! Just get rid of her!

4) Jessica Alba: She was bearable in the leading role in the post-apocalyptic TV show *Dark Angel*. At least we never had to see her abs, because it was too rainy in Seattle, where the show took place, for halter tops. Then along came a little film about an aspiring hip-hop dancer called *Honey, Sin City*, and *Fantastic Four*, and it was ALL ABS, ALL THE TIME for Miss Alba. Then her name started popping up in Eminem songs. Do we need this? Do we need the foremost poet of our time waxing eloquent on Jessica Alba? We do not. Get her out of here.

5) Halle Berry: Must I even go on? Oh, sure, she TRIED to look bad in *Monster's Ball*. Too bad it didn't work. Halle Berry could not look bad if her life depended on it. She seems to exist merely to make all the rest of us feel insecure. Bye-bye, Halle Berry.

6) Natalie Portman: I guess you WOULD need to cast someone really beautiful to play Princess Leia's mother. Still. Did they HAVE to cast someone so impossibly beautiful that she even makes those horrible lines in *Attack of the Clones* — the part where Amidala and Anakin are rolling down that hill with the stupid cow things — sound smart? Sure, Natalie's tried to redeem herself by playing indie roles that don't require vinyl bodysuits. But it doesn't matter how many colours you dye your hair, Ms Portman. We still think you're too pretty to live.

7) Shannyn Sossamon: I had my doubts in *A Knight's Tale*. I was like, What's someone that gorgeous doing living in the Middle Ages? But when I saw *The Rules of Attraction*, I KNEW: Shannyn Sossamon is way too beautiful to play a girl guys are dumping and cheating on all over the place. It would NEVER HAPPEN. Get rid of her!

8) Thandie Newton: I could handle her in the Audrey Hepburn role in *The Truth About Charlie*, the remake of *Charade*, because Audrey Hepburn was also too beautiful to live, so it was only to be expected that an actress playing a role she made famous would have to be that beautiful as well. And I could handle her in the sci-fi adventure *The Chronicles of Riddick*, because, basically, she played an alien. But when she showed up as Dr Carter's love interest on *ER*, I knew it was time: Time to get rid of her! What is Thandie Newton doing on TV? She is way too pretty to be on TV! She needs to stick to feature films! And no way would some doctor from Chicago go to the Congo and come back with THANDIE NEWTON. OK??? Women who look like her DON'T GO TO THE CONGO. Please get her out of my sight!

9) Nicole Kidman: OK, what is Nicole Kidman supposed to be? Is she supposed to be a human being? Because I think she might be one of those aliens that popped out of its human suit in the movie *Cocoon*. Remember, the super-shiny one? Because Nicole radiates beauty and light the same way that alien did. Hey, maybe she's one of those aliens the Scientologists are waiting for, the ones who are supposedly going to come back to rescue us all (well, at least all their fellow Scientologists) before we destroy our planet by abusing its natural resources. Maybe that's why Tom Cruise married her. Nicole Kidman, phone home! Tell the spaceship to hurry up!

10) Penelope Cruz: Another alien! Although she isn't as shiny as Nicole, Penelope is definitely too beautiful to be a human being. Maybe that's why Tom Cruise went out with her for so long! He THOUGHT she might be an alien, like Nicole, but then it turned out Penelope had simply won the genetic lottery, and is just naturally gorgeous. What's going to happen when Tom finds out that Katie Holmes isn't an alien either? Is he going to dump her too? HOW MANY MORE PRETERNATURALLY BEAUTIFUL WOMEN ARE LEFT FOR TOM TO MARRY/DATE? Why won't the Scientology mother ship hurry up and come and TAKE THEM ALL AWAY?????

Thursday, March 4, French

Whatever. That was so not helpful.

Détente – any international situation where previously hostile nations not involved in an open war warm up to each other and threats de-escalate.

God, it would rule if what Lana wanted was détente.

Thursday, March 4, Third-floor Stairwell

OK, so I'm here, but Lana's not.

She said after lunch. I'm sure that's what she said.

It's after lunch now.

SO WHERE IS SHE????

God, I HATE this sneaking around. It was SO HARD ditching those guys. I mean not Lilly, since she was meeting with Ms Martinez. But I mean Tina and Boris and Perin and everybody. I had to tell them I was coming up here to make a private phone call to Michael.

Which Tina so obviously thought meant I was coming up here to break the news to Michael that I'm not a party girl. She kept going, 'You go, girl!' until Shameeka was all, 'What are you guys TALKING about?'

Tina IS right, though. I've got to stop lying to Michael and tell him the truth. Only I've got to figure out a way to tell him that doesn't give away my dark secret – that I am not a party girl.

But HOW??? How to accomplish this? You would think, for an inveterate liar like myself, it would be easy to make up some excuse that would put me in the clear . . . like that I have to go to some special royal function this weekend.

Too bad no royals have died lately. A state funeral would be a PERFECT excuse.

But since no one's croaked recently, what about . . . a WEDDING?

Yeah! I could say one of my Grimaldi cousins is getting married again and I HAVE to go. Michael would believe me, it's not like he reads any of the magazines that would cover news like that . . . unless he tries looking it up on Netscape.

Maybe I'll just text him. Yeah, I'll text him right now, and be all, SRY, HAVE 2 GO 2 GENOVIA 4 THE WEEKEND! 2 BAD! DUTY CALLS! MAYBE NXT TIME!

Except that ultimately, it would be simpler if I just stopped lying. I mean, pretty soon I'm not going to be able to keep track of all my stories and get mixed up and—

SOMEONE IS COMING!!!!

It's LANA!!!!

Thursday, March 4, G and T

OK. So that was surreal.

So it WAS the money. That we're out of it, I mean. That's what Lana had meant when she'd said she knew.

And all she ended up wanting in exchange for her silence was to be invited to Grandmere's party. The one she's throwing to raise money for the Genovian olive farmers.

Seriously.

I was so shocked – I mean, I'd really expected Lana to ask me for something that would complicate my life a LOT more than a simple party invitation – that I was all, 'Why would you want to go to THAT? I mean – do YOU want to meet Bob Dylan too?'

Lana just looked at me like I'm stupid (so what else is new?) and went, 'Um, no. But Colin Farrell is going to be there. He's bidding on Ireland. *Everyone* knows that.'

Everyone except me, apparently.

But still. I pretended like I'd known. I went, 'Oh. Right. Sure. Yeah. OK.'

Then I said I'd make sure she got an invitation.

'TWO invitations,' Lana hissed, in a manner not dissimilar to the way Gollum went around hissing 'My precious' in *Lord of the Rings*. 'Trish wants to come too.'

Trisha Hayes is Lana's main henchperson, the Igor to her Dr Frankenstein. 'Though if she thinks SHE'S getting Colin, she's high.'

I didn't comment on this apparent rift in their unconditional sisterly love for one another. Instead, I was all, 'Um, yeah, OK, two invitations.'

But then, because I am incapable of keeping my

mouth shut, I was like, 'But, um, if you don't mind my asking – how'd you hear? About the money, I mean?'

She made another face and went, 'I looked up how much those stupid "cans and battles" recycling bins cost online. Then I just did some math. And I knew you had to be broke.'

God. Lana is even more conniving than I ever gave her credit for. Conniving AND much better at math than I am.

Maybe she SHOULD have been president.

I probably should have just let her go at that point. I probably should have just been all, 'Well, see ya.'

But I couldn't, of course. Because that would have been too easy. Instead, I had to be all, 'Um, Lana. Can I ask you a question?'

And she was like, 'What?' with her eyes all narrowed.

I couldn't believe the words that came out of my mouth next: 'How do you, um. Party?'

Lana's super-lipglossed mouth fell open at that one. 'How do you WHAT?'

'You know,' I said. 'Party. I mean, I know you go to a lot of, um, parties. So I was just wondering . . . like, what do you DO at them? How do you, you know. Party?'

Lana just shook her head, her stick-straight blonde hair (she's never had to worry about her hair forming an upside-down Yield sign-shape) shimmering under the fluorescent lights.

'God,' she said. 'You are such a retard.'

Since this was unchallengingly true, I didn't say anything.

This was apparently the right move, since Lana continued, 'You just show up – looking fantastic, of course.

Then you grab a beer. If the music's any good, you dance. If there's a hot guy, you hook up. That's it.'

I thought about this. 'I don't like beer,' I said.

But Lana just ignored me. 'And you wear something sexy.' Her gaze flicked from my combat boots up to the top of my head, and she added, 'Although for you, that might be a challenge.'

Then she sauntered off.

It can't be that simple. Partying, I mean. You just go, drink, dance, and, um, hook up? This information does not help me at all. What do you do if they're playing fast music? Are you supposed to dance fast? I look like I'm having a seizure when I dance fast.

And what are you supposed to do with this alleged beer while you're dancing? Do you put it down on like a coffee table or something? Or do you hold it while you dance? If you're dancing fast, won't it spill?

And don't you have to introduce yourself to everyone in the room? Grandmere insists that at parties I make sure I greet every guest personally, shaking their hand and enquiring after their health. Lana didn't say anything about that.

Or about the most important thing of all: What are you supposed to do about your bodyguard?

God. This partying thing is going to be even harder than I thought.

Thursday, March 4, Geometry

Something horrible just occurred to me. I mean, something even more horrible than the usual things that occur to me, like that Rocky might be suffering from childhood disintegrative disorder, or that the mole on my right hip is growing and could turn into a two hundred pound tumour like the one that grew on the lady I saw on that documentary on the Discovery Channel called *Two Hundred Pound Tumor*.

And that's that Lana might be self-actualized.

Seriously. I mean, that shakedown in the stairwell just now – that was almost a beautiful thing. It was CLASSIC.

And OK, she did it in a totally underhanded and manipulative way. But she got exactly what she set out to get.

She CAN'T be self-actualized. I mean, it totally wouldn't be fair if she was.

But you can't deny that she knows how to get what she wants out of life. Whereas I am just floundering around, lying to everyone all the time, and definitely NOT getting what I want.

I don't know. I mean, sure, she's pure unadulterated evil.

But it's something to think about.

Alternate exterior angles – A pair of angles on the outer sides of two lines cut by a transversal, but on opposite sides of the transversal.

Thursday, March 4, Earth Science

Just now Kenny asked me if I would re-copy our viscosity lab handout. He got Alfredo sauce all over it while filling in the blanks last night during dinner.

I guess it's a small price to pay for not actually having to know what viscosity is.

Homework:

Homeroom: N/A
PE: WASH GYM SHORTS!!!
US Economics: questions at end of Chapter 8
English: pages 133–154, *O Pioneers!*
French: rewrite *histoire*
G and T: cut black velvet knee-length skirt to micromini for party. FIND BERET!!!!
Geometry: Chapter 17, problems on pages 224–230
Earth Science: who cares? Kenny will do it

Thursday, March 4, the Grand Ballroom, the Plaza

A lot of people showed up for the *Braid!* auditions. I mean, a LOT.

Which is weird when you consider that none of the Drama Club people can even audition for *Braid!* because they're too busy rehearsing for *Hair*.

Which means that all the people who showed up today were theatre neophytes (which means beginner or novice according to Lilly), like Lilly and Tina and Boris and Ling Su and Perin (but not Shameeka, since she's only allowed that one extra-curricular per semester).

But Kenny was there, with some of his wonder-geek pals. And Amber Cheeseman, her school uniform's sleeves rolled up to show off her ape-like forearms.

Even the Guy Who Hates It When They Put Corn In The Chilli showed up.

Wow. I really had no idea there were so many aspiring thespians at AEHS.

Although if you think about it, acting *is* one of the few professions where you can make a ton of money while having no actual intelligence or talent whatsoever, as many a star has shown us.

So in that way you can see why it would be such an appealing career option to so many people.

Grandmere decided to actually run this as if it was a real audition. She had her maid hand out applications to everyone who walked through the door. We were supposed to fill them out, then stand for a Polaroid taken by Grandmere's chauffeur, then hand the Polaroid and our application to a tiny, extremely ancient man with huge glasses and a cravat, sitting behind a long table set Jennifer-Lopez-in-her-*Flashdance*-recreation-video-for-

'I'm Glad' style in the middle of the room. Grandmere sat next to him, with her miniature poodle, Rommel, shivering – in spite of his purple suede bomber jacket – on her lap.

I went up to her, waving my form and the Number One Noodle Son bag in which I had stowed her birthday gift earlier that day and dragged with me to school.

'I'm not filling this out,' I informed her, slapping the form down on the desk. 'Here's your present. Happy birthday.'

Grandmere took the bag from me – inside it were the padded satin hangers I had specially ordered from Chanel for her (whatever. Dad was the one who'd suggested – and paid – for them) – and said, 'Thank you. Please be seated, Amelia, dear.'

I knew the 'dear' was entirely for the benefit of the guy sitting next to her, whoever he was, not for me.

'I can't believe you're doing this,' I said to her. 'I mean . . . is this really how you want to spend your birthday?'

Grandmere just waved me away. 'When you're my age, Amelia,' she said, 'age becomes meaningless.'

Oh, whatever. She's in her SIXTIES, not her nineties. Instead of satin hangers, I should have got her one of those shirts I saw downtown that say DRAMA QUEEN inside the Dairy Queen logo.

Lilly flagged me down, so I sat with her and Tina and everybody. Right away Lilly was all, 'So what's the deal here, POG? I'm reporting on this for *The Atom*, so make it good.'

Lilly always gets the best assignments for the school paper. I have totally sunk to special features – i.e. occasional stories on the school band concert or the library's most recent acquisitions – since I am too busy with presidential and princess stuff to make a regular deadline.

'I don't know,' I said. 'I guess I'll find out when you find out.'

'Off the record,' Lilly said. 'Come on. Who's the little dude with the glasses?'

Before she could ask me anything else though, Grandmere stood up – dumping poor Rommel from her lap to the ballroom floor, where he slid around a bit before finding his footing on the slippery parquet – and said, in a deceptively kind voice (deceptive because of course Grandmere isn't kind), as the room fell silent, 'Welcome. For those of you who don't know, I am Clarisse, Dowager Princess of Genovia. I am very delighted to see so many of you here today for what will prove, I am certain, to be an important and historic moment in the history of Albert Einstein High School, and the theatrical world. But before I say more about that, allow me to introduce, without further ado, the much celebrated, world-famous theatrical director, Señor Eduardo Fuentes.'

Señor Eduardo! No! It can't be!

And yet . . . it was! It was the famous director who had asked Grandmere, all those years before, to come to New York with him and star in an original Broadway production!

He had to have been in his thirties back then. He's gotta be about a HUNDRED now. He's so old, he looks like a cross between Larry King and a raisin.

Señor Eduardo struggled to rise from his chair, but he was so rickety and frail that he only managed to get about a quarter of the way up before Grandmere pushed him down again impatiently, then went on with her

108

speech. I could practically hear his fragile bones snap under her grip.

'Señor Eduardo has directed countless plays and musicals on numerous prestigious stages worldwide, including Broadway and London's West End,' Grandmere informed us. 'You should all feel extremely honoured at the prospect of working with such an accomplished and revered professional.'

'Tank you,' Señor Eduardo managed to get in, waving his hands around and blinking in the bright lights from the ballroom ceiling. 'I tank you very, very much. It geeves me great pleasure to look out across so many youthful faces, shining with excitement and—'

But Grandmere wasn't letting anyone, not even an ancient world-famous director, steal her show.

'Ladies and gentlemen,' she cut him off, 'you are, as I said, about to audition for an original work that has never been performed before. If you are cast in this piece, you will, in essence, become a part of history. I am especially pleased about welcoming you here today because the piece you are about to read from was written almost entirely by –' she lowered her false eyelashes modestly '– me.'

'Oh, this is good,' Lilly said, eagerly jotting this down on her reporter's notebook. 'Are you getting this, POG?'

Oh, I was getting it all right. Grandmere wrote a PLAY? A play she means for us to put on to raise money for AEHS's senior graduation?

I am so, so dead.

'This piece,' Grandmere was going on, holding up a sheaf of papers – the script, apparently – 'is a work of complete originality and, I am not embarrassed to say, genius. *Braid!* is, essentially, a classic love story about a couple who must overcome extraordinary odds in order to be together. What makes *Braid!* all the more compelling is that it is based on historical fact. Everything that happens in this piece ACTUALLY HAPPENED IN REAL LIFE. Yes! *Braid!* is the story of an extraordinary young woman who, though she spent most of her life as a simple commoner, was one day thrust into a role of leadership. Yes, she was asked to assume the throne of a little country you all might have heard of: Genovia. This brave young woman's name? Why, none other than the great –'

No. Oh, my God, no. For the love of God, no. Grandmere's written a play about me. About MY LIFE. I AM GOING TO DIE. I AM GOING TO—

'– Rosagunde.'

Wait. What? ROSAGUNDE?

'Yes,' Grandmere went on. 'Rosagunde, the current princess of Genovia's great-great-great-great and so on grandmother, who exhibited incredible bravery in the face of adversity and was eventually rewarded for her efforts with the throne of what is today Genovia.'

Oh. My. God.

Grandmere's written a PLAY based on the story of my ancestress, Rosagunde.

AND SHE WANTS MY SCHOOL TO PUT IT ON.

IN FRONT OF EVERYONE.

'*Braid!* is, at heart, a love story. But the tale of the great Rosagunde is much more than a romance. It is, in fact –' here Grandmere paused, as much for dramatic effect as to take a sip from the glass on the table beside her. Water? Or straight vodka? We will never know. Not unless I had gone up there and taken a big swig – 'a MUSICAL.'

Oh. My. God.

Grandmere's written a MUSICAL based on the story of my ancestress, Rosagunde.

The thing is, I love musicals. *Beauty and the Beast* is like my favourite Broadway show of all time, and it's a musical.

But it is a musical about a prince who is under a curse and the bookish beauty who grows to love him anyway.

It is NOT about a feudal warmonger and the girl who strangles him to death.

Apparently, I was not the only one to realize this, since Lilly's hand shot up and she called, 'Excuse me.'

Grandmere looked startled. She isn't used to being interrupted once she gets going on one of her speeches.

'Please hold all questions until the end,' Grandmere said confusedly.

'Your Majesty,' Lilly said, ignoring her request. 'Is what you're telling us that this show, *Braid!*, is actually the story of Mia's great-great-great and so on grandmother, Rosagunde, who, in the year AD 568, was forced to wed the Visigothic warlord Alboin who conquered Italy and claimed it as his own?'

Grandmere bristled, the way Fat Louie does whenever I run out of Flaked Chicken and Tuna and have to give him some other flavour food, like Turkey Giblets, instead.

'That is *exactly* what I am trying to tell you,' Grandmere said stiffly. 'If you will allow me to continue.'

'Yeah,' Lilly said. 'But a MUSICAL? About a woman who is forced to marry a man who not only murders her father, but on their wedding night makes her drink from her dad's skull, and so consequently she murders him in

111

his sleep? I mean, isn't that kind of material a little bit HEAVY for a musical?'

'And a musical set in a military base during World War Two isn't a bit HEAVY? I believe they chose to call that one *South Pacific*,' Grandmere said with an arched brow. 'Or a musical about urban gang warfare in New York City during the fifties? *West Side Story*, I believe that one was called . . .'

Everyone in the room started murmuring – everyone except Señor Eduardo, who appeared to have dozed off. I had never thought about it before, but Grandmere *was* kind of right. A lot of musicals have pretty serious undertones, if you take the time to examine them. I mean, if you wanted to, you could say that *Beauty and the Beast* is about a hideously warped chimera who kidnaps and holds hostage a young peasant girl.

Trust Grandmere to destroy the one story I have ever wholeheartedly loved.

'Or even,' Grandmere went on above everyone's whispers, 'perhaps, a musical about the crucifixion of a man from Galilee . . . a little something called *Jesus Christ Superstar*?'

Gasps could be heard throughout the ballroom. Grandmere had scored a coup de grâce, and knew it. She had them eating out of the palm of her hand.

All but Lilly.

'Excuse me,' Lilly said again. 'But exactly when is this, erm, *musical* going to be performed?'

It was only then that Grandmere looked slightly – just slightly – uncomfortable.

'A week from today,' she said, with what I could tell was completely feigned self-assurance.

'But, Dowager Princess,' Lilly cried, above the gasps

and murmurs of all present – except Señor Eduardo, of course, who was still snoozing. 'You can't possibly expect the cast to memorize an entire show by next week. I mean, we're students – we have homework. I, personally, am the editor of the school literary magazine, which I intend to print Volume One, Issue One of next week. I can't do all that AND memorize an entire play.'

'Musical,' whispered Tina.

'Musical,' Lilly corrected herself. 'I mean, if I get in. That's – that's IMPOSSIBLE!'

'*Nothing* is impossible,' Grandmere assured us. 'Can you imagine what would have happened if the late John F. Kennedy had said it was *impossible* for man to walk on the moon? Or if Gorbachev had said it was *impossible* to take down the Berlin Wall? Or if, when my late husband invited the King of Spain and ten of his golfing partners to a state dinner at the last minute, I had said *Impossible*? It would have been an international incident! But the word impossible is not in my vocabulary. I had the major-domo set eleven more places, the cook add water to the soup, and the pastry chef whip up eleven more soufflés. And the party was such a huge success that the king and his friends stayed on for three more nights, and lost hundreds and thousands of dollars at the baccarat tables – all of which went to help poor, starving orphans all over Genovia.' I don't know what Grandmere is talking about. There are no starving orphans in Genovia. There weren't any during my grandfather's reign either. But whatever.

'And did I mention,' Grandmere asked, her gaze darting around the ballroom for some sympathetic faces, 'that you will be receiving one hundred extra credit

English points for taking part in this show? I have already settled it with your principal.'

The buzzing, which had been doubtful in tone, suddenly turned excited. Amber Cheeseman, who'd got up to leave – apparently due to the short amount of time the cast would have to learn their parts – hesitated, turned around, and came back to her seat.

'Lovely,' Grandmere said, positively beaming at this. 'Now. Shall we begin the audition process?'

'A musical about a woman who strangles her father's murderer with her hair,' Lilly muttered to herself, as she jotted in her notebook. 'Now I've seen everything.'

She wasn't the only one who seemed perturbed. Señor Eduardo looked pretty upset as well.

Oh, no, wait. He was just adjusting his oxygen hose.

'The roles that need filling most crucially are, of course, the leads Rosagunde and the foul warlord she dispatches with her hair, Alboin,' Grandmere continued. 'But there are also the parts of Rosagunde's father, her maid, the King of Italy, Alboin's jealous mistress, and of course Rosagunde's brave lover, the smithy, Gustav.'

Wait a minute. Rosagunde had a lover? How come no Genovian history book I've read before now has ever mentioned this?

And where was he, anyway, when his girlfriend was killing one of the most brutal sociopaths ever to have lived?

'So without further ado,' Grandmere exclaimed, 'let us begin the auditions!' She reached out and picked up two of the applications, with the Polaroids attached, not even glancing at Señor Eduardo, who was snoring lightly.

'Will a Kenneth
Cheeseman please ta

Only, of course,
moment of confu
figure out where
spot in front of
dozing and Ro

'Gustav,' s
Then: 'Rosa

'Now,' G

Lilly, besi
not to laugh out lou
so funny about the situati

Although when Kenny sta
Rosagunde! For though tonight you
body to him, I know your heart belongs to h
sort of see why she was laughing.

I ESPECIALLY saw why she was laughing when we
got to the musical part of the audition, and Kenny was
asked to sing a song of his choice – accompanied by a guy
playing the grand piano in the corner – and he chose to
sing 'Baby Got Back' by Sir Mix-a-Lot. There was just
something about him singing, 'Shake it, shake it, shake
that healthy butt,' that made me laugh until tears
streamed down my face (though I had to do it super
quietly, so no one would notice).

It got even worse when Grandmere said, 'Erm, thank
you for that, young man,' and it was Amber's turn to
sing, because the song she chose to sing was Celine
Dion's 'My Heart Will Go On', from *Titanic*, a song to
which Lilly has designed a dance she does with her
fingers, based on the Las Vegas hotel Bellagio's 'water
dance' to the same song, which is performed almost

…n in front of the hotel's drive-

…nt of tourists strolling down the

… hard (albeit silently) that I didn't
…ne of the girl Grandmere called next
…ne part of Rosagunde.

… until Lilly poked me with one of her danc-

… Thermopolis Renaldo, please?' Grandmere

… try, Grandmere,' I called from my seat. 'But I
… turn in a sheet. Remember?'

Grandmere gave me the evil eye as everyone else
…cked in their breath.

'Why are you here then,' she enquired acidly, 'if you didn't plan to audition?'

Um, because I have been meeting with you at the Plaza every day after school for the past year and a half, remember?

What I said instead was, 'I'm just here to support my friends.'

To which Grandmere merely replied, 'Do not trifle with me, Amelia. I haven't the time nor the patience. Get up here. Now.'

She said it in her most dowager-princessy voice – a voice I totally recognized. It was the same voice she uses right before she drags out some excruciatingly embarrassing story from my childhood to mortify me in front of everyone – like the time I accidentally smacked my chest into the rear-view mirror of the limo while I was Rollerblading in the driveway of her chateau, Miragnac, and I noticed afterwards it was all swollen and I showed my dad and he was like, 'Um, Mia, I don't think that's swelling. I think you're getting breasts,' and Grandmere told every single person she met for the rest of my stay that her granddaughter mistook her own breasts for contusions.

Which if you think about it isn't THAT bad of a mistake to make, since they aren't much bigger today than they were then.

I could totally see her, however, trotting out this story in front of everyone if I didn't do what she told me to.

'Fine,' I said, from between gritted teeth, and got up to audition just as Grandmere called the name of the next guy she wanted to hear read.

A guy who just happened to be named John Paul Reynolds-Abernathy the Fourth.

Who, when he stood up, turned out to be . . .

. . . The Guy Who Hates It When They Put Corn In The Chilli.

Thursday, March 4, in the Limo home

She denies it, of course. Grandmere, I mean. About just wanting to put on this play – excuse me, MUSICAL – to butter up John Paul Reynolds-Abernathy the Third by casting his kid in the lead.

But what other explanation is there? Am I REALLY supposed to believe she's just doing this to help me with my little financial problem, like she says, since people are supposedly going to pay admission to this little nightmare she's created, and I can use all the money to restore the student government's diminished coffers?

Yeah. Right.

I fully confronted her as soon as the auditions were over.

'How am I embarrassing you this time, Amelia?' she wanted to know, after everyone had left and it was just her and me and Lars and the rest of her staff – and Rommel and Señor Eduardo, of course. But both of them were asleep. It was hard to tell whose snores were louder.

'Because you're going to give –' I almost called him the *Guy Who Hates It When They Put Corn In The Chilli*, but stopped myself just in time – 'John Paul Reynolds-Abernathy the Fourth the lead in your play just so his dad will feel like he owes you one and possibly drop his bid on the faux island of Genovia! I KNOW what you're up to, Grandmere. I'm taking US Economics this semester, I know all about scarcity and utility. Admit it!'

'*Braid!* is a musical, not a play,' is all Grandmere would say about that.

But she didn't HAVE to say more. Her very silence is

an admission of guilt! John Paul Reynolds-Abernathy the Fourth is being used!

Granted, he doesn't seem to know it. Or, if he does, he doesn't exactly seem to mind. Strangely, away from the overuse of farinaceous grains in the AEHS cafeteria, the Guy Who Hates It When They Put Corn In The Chilli seems pretty happy-go-lucky. 'J.P.' – as he asked Grandmere to call him – is almost menacingly large (not unlike the bodyguard, played by Adam No-Relation-to-Alec Baldwin, in the low-budget high-school bully film, *My Bodyguard*) at six foot two at least. His floppy brown hair looks less shaggy and much shinier when it's not under the harsh glow of the cafeteria's less-than-flattering lighting.

And up close, it turns out, J.P. has surprisingly bright blue eyes.

I got to see them – J.P.'s eyes – up close because Grandmere made us do the scene where Rosagunde has just strangled Alboin and is freaking out about it when Gustav comes bursting into the bedroom to rescue his lady love from a ravishing by her new husband, not realizing she'd

a) already drunk the guy under the table so he couldn't get it up to ravish her in the first place, and
b) killed him after he passed out from all the Genovian grappa he'd consumed.

But, oh well. Better late than never.

I have no idea why Grandmere made me go through that farce of an audition, since it's clear she's going to cast J.P. as Gustav – just to appease his dad. Although, truthfully, J.P. was really good, both with the acting AND the singing (he did a totally hilarious rendition of 'The Safety Dance' by Men Without Hats) – and Lilly as Rosagunde. I mean, Lilly was clearly the best out of the all the girls (her version of Garbage's 'Bad Boyfriend' nearly brought the house down) and has the most experience with the whole performance thing, on account of her TV show and all.

Plus she was really good at killing Alboin – which is only natural, since if there's anyone at AEHS who I could see strangling someone with a braid, it's Lilly. Oh, and maybe Amber Cheeseman.

But the whole time it was my turn to audition, Grandmere kept yelling, 'Enunciate, Amelia!' and 'Don't turn your back to your audience, Amelia! Your behind is not as expressive as your face!' (which caused no small amount of chortling from the side of the room my friends were sitting on).

And she didn't seem at ALL impressed by my version of 'Barbie Girl' by Aqua (especially the chorus, *Come on, Barbie/Let's go party*, which if you think about it is highly ironic, considering my inability to do so. Party, I mean), even though I have secretly been practising this song in my room for months in preparation for just this sort of event – well, OK, for a possible 'sing-off' with some girl from Michael's dorm during their monthly lip-sync in the caff.

I mean, it's not as if Grandmere's going to cast me, so why all the yelling? I mean, what do I even know about acting? Apart from a brief stint as the mouse in *The Lion and the Mouse* in the fourth grade, I am not exactly what you'd call experienced in the dramatic arts.

It was a total relief when Grandmere finally let me sit down.

Then, on our way back to our seats, J.P. said, 'Hey, that was fun, huh?' to me.

AND I DIDN'T SAY ANYTHING BACK!!!!!!!!!!!

BECAUSE I WAS SO STUNNED!!!!!!!

Because to me, J.P. is the Guy Who Hates It When They Put Corn In The Chilli. He's not John Paul Reynolds-Abernathy the Fourth. The Guy Who Hates It When They Put Corn In The Chilli doesn't have a NAME. He's just . . . the Guy Who Hates It When They Put Corn In The Chilli. The guy I wrote a short story about. A short story that was rejected by *Sixteen* magazine. A short story I hope to expand into a novel someday.

A short story at the end of which the Guy Who Hates It When They Put Corn In The Chilli throws himself under the F train.

How can I *talk* to a guy I had throw himself under a train – even if it WAS only fiction?

Worse, on her way out after the auditions were over, Tina (Jessica Simpson's 'With You') was all, 'Hey, you know what? The Guy Who Hates It When They Put Corn In The Chilli is kinda cute. I mean, when he's not freaking out about corn.'

'Yeah,' Lilly agreed. 'Now that you mention it, he kinda is.'

I waited for Lilly to add something like, 'Too bad he's such a freak,' or, 'It's a shame about the corn thing.' But she didn't. SHE DIDN'T.

!!!!!!!!!!!!!!!!!!!!

My friends think the Guy Who Hates It When They

121

Put Corn In The Chilli is cute!!!! A guy I KILLED in my short story!

And it's all Grandmere's fault. If she hadn't got it into her head to buy a stupid faux island, it would never have occurred to her to write a musical – let alone put it on – for my school, and I never would have met the Guy Who Hates It When They Put Corn In The Chilli, much less found out that his name is J.P. and that, contrary to the character in my short story about him, he is NOT an existential loner, but actually just a nice guy who has a pretty good singing voice, and whom my friends think is cute (and they're right, he is).

God, I hate her.

Well, OK, it's wrong to hate people.

But I don't love her, let's put it that way. In fact, on the list of people I love, Grandmere isn't even in the top five.

PEOPLE I LOVE, IN ORDER OF HOW MUCH I LOVE THEM:

1. Fat Louie
2. Rocky
3. Michael
4. My mom
5. My dad
6. Lars
7. Lilly
8. Tina
9. Shameeka/Ling Su/Perin
10. Mr G
11. Pavlov, Michael's dog
12. The Drs Moscovitz

13. Tina Hakim Baba's little brothers and sisters
14. Mrs Holland, my government teacher last semester
15. Buffy the Vampire Slayer
16. Ronnie, our next-door neighbour
17. Boris Pelkowski
18. Principal Gupta
19. Rommel, Grandmere's dog
20. Kevin Bacon
21,000. Ms Martinez
22,000. The doorman at the Plaza who wouldn't let me in that one time because I wasn't dressed fancy enough
23,000. Trisha Hayes
24,000,000. Lana Weinberger
25,000,000,000. Grandmere

And I don't even feel the least bit bad about it. She brought it on HERSELF.

Thursday, March 4, the Loft

Guess what Mr G made for dinner tonight?
    Oh, yes. Chilli.
    There wasn't corn in it, but still.
    Maybe I should throw MYSELF under an F train.

Thursday, March 4, the Loft

I knew I'd be inundated with emails the minute I turned my computer on. And I was right.

From Lilly:

WomynRule: Does your grandmother realize that the subject matter of her little play is practically rated PG-13? I mean, it contains attempted rape, excessive alcohol consumption, murder, violence — about the only thing it DOESN'T have in it is bad language, and that's only because it takes place in the year 568. And could you believe how off-key Amber Cheeseman was? I totally blew her out of the water. If I don't get the part of Rosagunde, it will be a travesty of justice. I was MADE to play this role.

From Tina:

Iluvromance: That was fun today! I really hope I get the part of Rosagunde. I know I won't, because Lilly was so good at the audition the part will totally go to her. But it would be soo cool to play a princess. I mean,

125

not for you, since you play a princess in real life and everything. But for someone like me, I mean. I know Lilly will get it. Still, I hope I don't get the part of Alboin's mistress. I wouldn't want to play a mistress. Also, I don't think my dad would let me.

From Ling Su:

Painturgrl: OK, clearly Lilly is going to get the part of Rosagunde, but if I get stuck with the part of the mistress, I am going to scream! Asian actresses are always being relegated to roles where they are forced to play sexual subservients. Or, worse, just plain subservients . . . like Rosagunde's maid. I refuse to be typecast! I hope she didn't think my performance of Gwen Stefani's 'Hollaback Girl' was too strident. Also, is your grandma going to need help with the sets? Because I paint totally good castles and stuff.

From Perin:

IndigoGrlFan:Wasn't that fun today? I know I

wasn't very good. I was just so surprised, you know? I mean, that your grandmother had me read for the part of Gustav instead of Rosagunde. Especially after I sang TATU's 'Not Gonna Get Us'. But it must have been because there were so many more girls than boys auditioning. You don't think she thinks I'm a boy, do you???

From Boris:

JoshBell2: Mia, do you think your grand-mother would be willing to add a scene to her play where Gustav takes out a violin and serenades Rosagunde? Because I really think that would add some emotional depth to the production, should I be the person cast to play Gustav. Plus, it would add historical accuracy, since the rebec, the violin's predecessor, dates from 5,000 BC. I know Maroon 5's 'She Will Be Loved' wasn't the most inspired choice for my audition song, but Tina said she didn't think your grandmother would like the only other song I'd prepared —

Eminem's 'Cleanin' Out My Closet'.

From Kenny:

$E=mc^2$:   Mia, I'm troubled by the sugges-
              tion your grandmother made as I
              was sitting back down after my
              audition piece that whoever
              plays the part of Gustav the
              smithy ought at least to be
              capable of growing facial hair.
              It almost sounded as if she were
              inferring that I myself am not
              capable of this, when the truth
              is that I DO have facial hair, it
              is just very fair. I hope your
              grandmother is not going to be
              prejudiced against blonds in her
              casting of the male roles.

From Shameeka:

Beyonce_Is_Me: All anybody can talk about
                are those auditions today!
                Sounds like Lilly is going to
                get the lead (what else is
                new?). Wish I could have been
                there. Is it true the Guy Who
                Hates It When They Put Corn
                In The Chilli was there????

Seriously. It's like they've forgotten we have other things

to worry about besides who is going to be cast as Gustav and Rosagunde.

Like, for instance, the fact that we are still broke.

I guess it doesn't really matter so much to them, since they are not the ones in charge.

One thing I will say for Grandmere's choice of plays: she could not have chosen a piece that more fully illustrates the problems of the royal, in that, ultimately, you are all alone when it comes to making decisions of state. As it did for Rosagunde in that bedroom fifteen hundred years ago, the buck, for me, stops here.

This is all too much for one lone teen to bear. I need someone to help me, someone to tell me what the right thing to do is. Should I just come clean with Amber, confess my sin, and get my whupping over with?

Or is there still a chance I can get the money before she finds out?

It's times like these when I realize how woefully inadequate my familial support network really is. I mean, I can't turn to my mother for advice in this matter. She is the person who was responsible for our cable going out at least once a month because she forgot to pay the bill – at least, before Mr G moved in.

And I can't turn to my dad. If he finds out how badly I've screwed up my STUDENT government budget, he's not going to be exactly jazzed about turning me loose on our COUNTRY's budget. The last thing I need right now is a series of lectures from Dad on cost-effective municipal planning.

I already told Grandmere, and you can see the good THAT did. Who else is there for me to turn to, except Michael, of course?

And we all know how helpful HE was in the matter.

129

Speaking of Michael, the only email I got that was unrelated to today's *Braid!* audition was the one I got from him. And that's just because he doesn't even go to AEHS any more and didn't know anything about what was going on:

SkinnerBx: Hey, Thermopolis! How's it going? I was wondering if you wanted to come over tomorrow night for a sci-fi film-fest. I have to screen a bunch of them for my History of Dystopic Science Fiction in Film elective, and since I'm having the party Saturday night, I figured I should watch them while I had the chance. Want to join me?

It would have been inappropriate, of course, for me to say what I WANTED to say, which was: Michael, you are my life blood, my reason for living, the only thing that keeps me sane in the tempest-tossed sea of life, and I would like nothing better than to screen a bunch of dystopic sci-fi flicks with you tomorrow night.

Because it's lame to say that kind of stuff in an email. But I still thought it, in my head.

FtLouie: I'd love to.
>

SkinnerBx: Excellent. We can order in from Number One Noodle Son.
>

FtLouie: And I can make some dip.
>

130

```
SkinnerBx: Dip? What for?
>
FtLouie:   For the party! Don't people serve
           dip at parties?
>
SkinnerBx: Oh. Yeah. But I just figured I'd buy
           some Saturday afternoon, or what-
           ever.
```

I could see that my effort to appear enthusiastic about Michael's party had fallen completely flat. But I persevered nonetheless, because I couldn't let him know, you know, how NOT excited I was about it.

```
FtLouie:   Homemade dip is always better. I
           can make it and leave it overnight
           in the refrigerator, and that way
           it will be all gelled and every-
           thing for the party. Which I'm so
           excited about coming to.
>
SkinnerBx: Um. OK. Whatever you want. See you
           tomorrow then.
>
FtLouie:   Can't wait!
```

Actually, though, I CAN wait . . . both for the party AND the dystopic sci-fi film festival. Because those movies Michael has to watch for that class of his are MAJOR bummers. I mean, *Soylent Green*? Excuse me, but gross.

Plus a lot of them have very scary parts, and scary movies have completely screwed with my psyche.

Seriously. I think scary movies are responsible for half, if not more, of my neuroses.

TOP 20 WAYS SCARY MOVIES HAVE MESSED ME UP:

1) I can't see chairs pulled away from the table without thinking of *Poltergeist* and having to push them back in. Ditto drawers that have been pulled out.

2) I can't pass those red and white smokestacks across from the FDR without thinking about poor Mel Gibson in *Conspiracy Theory*.

3) I can't go over a bridge without thinking of *The Mothman Prophecies*. Ditto when I see a chemical plant.

4) After seeing *Blair Witch*, I can no longer go
   a) into wooded areas
   b) camping
   c) into any dark basements.

Not that I would have done any of those things anyway. But now I REALLY won't.

5) For a long time I couldn't look at the TV without thinking that a girl might crawl out of it and kill me like in *The Ring* and *The Ring Two*.

6) Every time I see an alley I expect there to be a dead body in it. But that's probably from too many episodes of *Law & Order*, not the movies.

132

7) Don't even talk to me about boiling pots of water on the stove (Whitey the rabbit from *Fatal Attraction*).

8) Little white dogs = Precious from *The Silence of the Lambs*.

9) Any super modern-looking, windowless building in the middle of nowhere is the place where they harvest the organs of people in comas from the movie *Coma*.

10) Cornfields = the movie *Signs*, and we're all going to die.

11) After *Titanic*, I will never, ever, ever, go on a cruise.

12) Whenever I see an oil tanker on the road, I know I'm going to die, because whenever you see one in the movies, it explodes.

13) If a semi is tailing us, I always assume it's trying to kill us, like in *Duel*.

14) I can't go through the Holland Tunnel without thinking it's going to leak like in *Daylight*.

15) I don't know if I will ever be able to have children thanks to *Rosemary's Baby*. I will definitely never live in the Dakota. I don't know how Yoko Ono stands it.

16) I'll never adopt, either, thanks to *The Good Son*.

17) I will never get anaesthesia for anything but non-elective surgery because of *She Woke Up Pregnant*.

18) After talking at length to several elevator repair-men, I know now that unless someone places an incendiary device on top of the elevator, like in *Speed*, it is mathematically impossible for all the cables supporting it to snap at once. Still. You never know.

19) Thanks to *Jaws* I will never set foot in the ocean again.

20) The call is ALWAYS coming from inside the house.

See? I have been SCREWED UP by the movies. The whole reason I hate parties, probably, is because of how traumatized I was over Broken Lizard's *Club Dread*, which I watched with Michael, thinking it was going to be a comedy, like *Super Troopers*. Only it turned out to be a horror film about young people being killed at a trop-ical resort, usually during a party.

Michael doesn't realize the MAJOR sacrifice I am making, just by agreeing to watch whatever it is he's going to make me watch tomorrow night.

In fact, probably one of the biggest reasons I haven't transcended my ego and achieved self-actualization yet is because of the psychological scarring I have received from the movies. I wonder if Dr Carl Jung knew about this when he invented self-actualization. Or did they even HAVE movies back when he was alive?

From the desk of
Her Royal Highness Princess Amelia Mignonette
Grimaldi Thermopolis Renaldo

Dear Dr Carl Jung,

Hi. I know you're still dead and all, but I was just wondering – when you were inventing the whole self-actualization thing, did you take into account the way movies mess people up? Because it is very difficult to transcend the ego when you are constantly thinking about things like oil tankers blowing up on the highway.

And what about teenagers? We have special concerns and insecurities that adults simply don't seem to possess. I mean, I have never seen a single adult worrying about a valedictorian possibly taking out a death warrant on her.

And what about boyfriends? There isn't a single mention of boyfriends or even romance on the branches of the Jungian tree of self-actualization. I understand that in order to reap the fruits of life (health, joy, contentment), you must start at the roots (compassion, charity, trust).

But can you really trust your boyfriend when, for instance, he is planning on having a party to which he is inviting college girls, who often smoke and seem routinely to refer to Nietzsche?

I'm not trying to criticize you or anything. I just really want to know. I mean, did you ever see *Coma*? It was really freaking scary. And I imagine if you ever saw it, you might revise some of your requirements for transcending the ego. Like, for instance, the whole trust thing. I mean, I know it's good to trust your doctor – up to a point.

But do you ever REALLY know that he's not purposely going to put you in a coma in order to harvest your organs and sell them to some really rich dude in Bolivia?

No. You don't. So see? There's a flaw in your whole theory.

So. What am I supposed to do now?

Still your friend,
Mia Thermopolis

Friday, March 5, the Limo on the way to school

If Lilly comments one more time on how her interpretation of Rosagunde is going to make Julia Roberts's portrayal of Erin Brockovich look like community theatre, my head is going to spin off, shoot through the sunroof and land in the East River.

Friday, March 5, Homeroom

They just announced over the intercom that the cast list for *Braid!* will go up outside the administrative offices at noon.

Just my luck. You could cut the tension around here like a knife. Not just the nervousness over who is going to get what part, either.

The Drama Club is hopping mad that someone is putting on a musical to rival theirs. They claim they are going to contact the writers of *Hair* and tell them what Grandmere is doing – you know, because her musical's name is so close to theirs.

I hope they do.

Although, if Grandmere gets sued and stops the show, I am back to selling candles again to raise the five grand I need.

On the other hand, there is no guarantee that a musical version of the story of my ancestress Rosagunde could even raise five thousand dollars in ticket sales in the first place. I mean, who would pay money to go to a show written by my grandma? She once gave a speech at a benefit to raise money for the Genovian version of the ASPCA about how the kindest thing you can do for an animal is immortalize it forever by skinning it and using its pelt as a lovely shrug or throw for a divan.

So you see where I am coming from about this.

Lana just asked me if I had her invitations yet. She asked me this as I was stepping into my underwear after my post-volleyball shower, which is about as vulnerable a position as a person can be in.

I said I hadn't had a chance to get them yet, but that I would.

Lana then looked down at my Jimmy Neutron underwear and went, 'Whatever, freak,' and walked away before I got a chance to explain to her that I wear Jimmy Neutron underwear because Jimmy reminds me a bit of my boyfriend.

The genius part. Not the hair.

But I guess maybe it's just as well. I highly doubt Lana would understand – even if she DID wear her boyfriend's soccer shorts under her school skirt.

Friday, March 5, US Economics

Demand = How much (quantity) of a product or service is desired by buyers.

Supply = How much the market can offer.

Equilibrium = When supply and demand are equal the economy is said to be in equilibrium. The amount of goods being supplied is exactly the same as the amount of goods being demanded.

Disequilibrium = This occurs whenever the price or quantity is not equal to demand/supply.

[So, basically, the student government of AEHS is currently in disequilibrium due to our funds (zero) not being equal to the demand for one night's rental of Alice Tully Hall ($5,728.00).]

Alfred Marshall, author of *The Principles of Economics* (circa 1890): 'Economics is on one side the study of wealth; and on the other, and more important side, a part of the study of man.'

Huh. So that sort of makes economics a SOCIAL science. Like psychology. Because it isn't really about numbers. It's about PEOPLE, and what they are willing to spend – or do – to get what they want.

   Like Lana, for instance. You know, how she was going to rat me out to Amber if I didn't get her those invitations to Grandmere's party?

   That was a classic example of supply (I had the

supply) versus demand (her demand that I give her what she wanted).

All of which leads me to believe that it's entirely possible that Lana Weinberger isn't self-actualized at all.

She's simply really good at economics!

Friday, March 5, English

One more period until the cast list goes up! Oh, I hope Boris gets the part of Gustav! He wants it so badly!

I hope he gets it, too, Tina! I hope everyone gets the parts they want.

What part do YOU want, Mia?

Me???? Nothing!!! I didn't even submit a photo or a form, remember?
I stink at that kind of thing. Acting and stuff, I mean.

Don't put yourself down like that! Your Ciara imitation has got really EXCELLENT. And I thought you were really good as Rosagunde! Don't you want the part just a little bit?

No, really. I'm a writer, not an actress. Remember??? I want to WRITE the things the people on stage say. Well, not really, because there's no actual money in playwrighting. But you get what I mean.

Oh. Right. That makes sense.

Well, all I can say is, if I don't get the part of Rosagunde, we'll all know it's because of the N word.

Nude scene???? When did you do a nude scene????

142

No, you idiot. NEPOTISM. Favouritism shown to a family member.

But that won't happen because Mia didn't really audition and doesn't even WANT a part. So you should be fine, Lilly! Gosh, I hope we all get the parts we want - even if that means NO part!

I'll second that!

CAST LIST FOR
Albert Einstein High School's
Alternative Spring Musical

Braid!

Chorus . . . . Amber Cheeseman, Julio
Juarez, Margaret Lee,
Eric Patel, Lauren
Pembroke, Robert
Sherman, Ling Su Wong
Rosagunde's father . . . Kenneth Showalter
Rosagunde's maid. . . . Tina Hakim Baba
King of Italy . . . . Perin Thomas
Alboin . . . . Boris Pelkowski
Alboin's mistress . . . . . Lilly Moscovitz
Gustav . . . . .John Paul Reynolds-
Abernathy IV
Rosagunde . . . . Amelia Thermopolis
Renaldo

FIRST REHEARSAL TODAY, 3.30 p.m.
The Plaza Hotel, Grand Ballroom

I know I'm only supposed to use my cellphone for emer-
gencies. But the minute I saw that cast list, I could tell
this was an emergency. A **MAJOR** one. Because

Grandmere has no idea of the MAGNITUDE of what she's done.

I called her from the Jet Line.

'Hello, you've reached Clarisse, Dowager Princess of Genovia. I'm either shopping or receiving a beauty treatment at the moment and cannot come to the phone. At the tone, please leave your name and number and I'll ring you back shortly.'

Boy, did I let her have it. Or her voicemail anyway:

'Grandmere! What do you think you're doing, casting me in your musical? You know I didn't even want to audition for it and that I don't have any acting talent whatsoever!'

Tina, in line beside me, kept nudging me, going, 'But your version of "Barbie Girl" is so good!'

'Well, OK, maybe I can sing,' I shouted into the phone, 'but Lilly is much better! You'd better call me back right away so we can get this mess straightened out, because you're making a HUGE mistake.' I added this last part for Lilly's sake, who, even though she's taken the whole thing really well, still looked a little red around the eyes when she joined us in the Jet Line, after having disappeared into the ladies' room for a long time once she'd seen the cast list.

'Don't worry,' I said to Lilly after I hung up. 'You're destined for the part of Rosagunde. Really.'

But Lilly pretended not to care. 'Whatever. It's not like I don't have enough to do. I don't know if I'd have had time to memorize all those lines anyway.'

Which is ridiculous, since Lilly practically has a photographic memory and almost a hundred per cent aural recall (which makes fighting with her super hard because sometimes she drags out stuff you said like five years before and have no memory of ever saying. But SHE remembers it. Perfectly).

It's just so wrong! If anyone deserves the lead in *Braid!*, it's her!

'At least by playing Alboin's mistress,' Lilly said all bravely, 'I only have a few lines – "Why would you marry her, who doesn't even want you, when you could have me, who adores you?" or whatever. So I'll have plenty of time to work on things that REALLY matter. Like *Fat Louie's Pink Butthole*.'

And OK, I feel really badly for Lilly, because she totally deserves the part of Rosagunde and all.

BUT I STILL HATE THAT NAME!!!

Friday, March 5, Later during lunch

So everyone is freaked out because on the way back to our table from the Jet Line I stopped by where J.P. was sitting by himself and asked him if he wanted to join us.

I don't know what the big deal is. I mean, it's not like I suddenly whipped off my clothes and started doing the hula in front of everyone. I just told a guy we know, who some of us may be spending a lot of time with in the near future, that he can come sit with us if he wants to.

And he said thanks.

And next thing I knew, John Paul Reynolds-Abernathy the Fourth was sliding his tray down next to mine.

'Oh, hi, J.P.,' Tina said. She shot a warning look at Boris, since he was the one who'd objected so strongly when I'd suggested inviting J.P. to join us, back when we'd only known him as the Guy Who Hates It When They Put Corn In The Chilli.

But Boris wisely refrained from saying anything about not wanting to eat with a corn hater.

'Thanks,' J.P. said, squeezing into the spot we made him at our table. Not that he's fat. He's just . . . big. You know, really tall, and everything.

'So what do you think of the falafel?' J.P. asked Lilly, who looked startled at being spoken to by a guy who, for the past two years, we've sort of mocked.

She looked even more startled when she realized they both had the exact same things on their trays: falafel, salad and Yoo-hoo chocolate drink.

'It's good,' she said, staring at him with kind of a funny look on her face. 'If you put enough tahini on it.'

147

'Anything's good,' J.P. said, 'if you put enough tahini on it.'

THIS IS SO TRUE!!!!!

Trust Boris to go, 'Even corn?' all mock-innocently.

Tina shot him another warning look . . .

. . . but it was too late. The damage was done. Boris was clearly unable to restrain himself. He started smirking into a napkin, while pretending to blow his nose.

'Well,' J.P. said, cheerfully falling for the bait. 'I don't know about that. But maybe, like, erasers.'

Perin brightened at this statement.

'I've always thought erasers would taste good fried,' she said. 'I mean, sometimes, when I have calamari, that's what it reminds me of. Fried erasers. So I bet they'd taste good with tahini on them too.'

'Oh, sure,' J.P. said. 'Fry anything, it'd taste good. I'd eat one of these napkins if it was fried.'

Tina, Lilly, and I exchanged surprised looks. J.P., it turns out, is kind of . . . funny.

Like, in a humorous, not strange, way.

'My grandmother makes fried grasshopper sometimes,' Ling Su volunteered. 'It's pretty good.'

'See,' J.P. said. 'Told you.' Then, looking at me, he went, 'What're you working on so diligently over there, Mia? Something due next period?'

'Don't mind her,' Lilly said with a snort. 'She's just writing in her journal. As usual.'

'Is that what that is?' J.P. said. 'I always kinda wondered.' Then, when I threw him a questioning look, he went, 'Well, every time I see you, you've got your nose buried in that notebook.'

Which can mean only one thing: the whole time we've

148

been watching the Guy Who Hates It When They Put Corn In The Chilli, he's been watching us right back!

Even freakier, he opened his backpack and pulled out a Mead wide-ruled composition notebook with a black marbled cover with *KEEP OUT! PRIVATE!* written all over it.

JUST LIKE MINE!!!!!!!!!!!!!!!!!!!!

'I too am a fan of the Mead composition notebook,' he explained. 'Only I don't keep a journal in mine.'

'What's in it then?' Lilly, always ready to ask prying questions, enquired.

J.P. looked slightly embarrassed.

'Oh, I just do some creative writing from time to time. Well, I mean, I don't know how creative it is. But, you know. Whatever. I try.'

Lilly asked him immediately if he had anything he'd like to contribute to the first issue of *Fat Louie's Pink Butthole*. He flipped through a couple of pages, and then asked, 'How about this?' and read aloud:

Silent Movie
By J. P. Reynolds-Abernathy IV

All the time we're being seen
By Gupta's silent surveillance machine.
What type of fly needs so many eyes?
Every turn of a hallway another surprise.

Gupta's security is not so secure
Since we know it's based on nothing but fear.
If I had my way, I would not be here
Except that my tuition's paid to the end of the year.

Wow. I mean . . . WOW. That was like . . . totally good. I don't really get it, but I think it's about, like, the security cameras, and how Principal Gupta thinks she knows everything about us, but she doesn't. Or something.

Actually, I don't know what it's about. But it must be good, because even Lilly seemed really impressed. She tried to get J.P. to submit it to *Fat Louie's Pink Butthole*. She thinks it might bring down the entire administration.

God. It's not often you meet a boy who can write poetry. Or can even read anything. Beyond the instructions on an Xbox, I mean.

How weird to think that the Guy Who Hates It When They Put Corn In The Chilli is a writer like me. What if the whole time I've been writing short stories about J.P., he's been writing short stories about ME? Like, what if HE's written a story called 'No More Beef!' about the time they put meat in the vegetarian lasagne and I accidentally ate some and threw that giant fit?

God. That would kind of . . . suck.

Friday, March 5, G and T

Grandmere called back right as the bell signalling the end of lunch started ringing.

'Amelia,' she said prissily. 'You wanted me for something?'

'Grandmere, what are you doing, casting me in your musical?' I demanded. 'You know I don't want to be in it. I didn't fill out the audition form, remember?'

'Is that all?' Grandmere seemed disappointed. 'I thought you were only supposed to use your mobile in cases of emergency. I hardly think this constitutes an emergency, Amelia.'

'Well, you're wrong,' I informed her. 'This IS an emergency. An emergency crisis in our relationship – yours and mine.'

Grandmere seemed to find this statement totally hilarious.

'Amelia,' she said. 'What is the one thing you have been complaining about most since the day you discovered you were, in reality, a princess?'

I had to think about this one.

'Having a bodyguard follow me around?' I asked in a whisper, so Lars wouldn't overhear and get his feelings hurt.

'What else?'

'Not being able to go anywhere without the paparazzi stalking me?'

'Think again.'

'The fact I have to spend my summers attending meetings of Parliament instead of going to camp like my friends?'

'Princess lessons, Amelia,' Grandmere says into the phone. 'You loathe and despise them. Well, guess what?'

'What?'

'Princess lessons are cancelled for the duration of rehearsals for *Braid!*. What do you think of that?'

You could almost hear the smug satisfaction in her voice. She totally thought she'd pulled one over on me.

Little did she know that my loyalty to my friends is stronger than my hatred for princess lessons!

'Nice try,' I informed her. 'But I'd rather have to learn to say *Please pass the butter* in fifty thousand languages than see Lilly not get the part she deserves.'

'Lilly is unhappy with the part she received?' Grandmere asked.

'Yes! She's the best actress of all of us, she should have had the lead! But you gave her the stupid part of Alboin's mistress and she only has like two lines!'

'There are no small parts in the theatre, Amelia,' Grandmere said. 'Only small actors.'

WHAT? I had no idea what she was talking about.

'Whatever, Grandmere,' I said. 'If you don't want your show to suck, you should have cast Lilly in the lead. She—'

'Did I mention,' Grandmere interrupted, 'how much I enjoyed meeting your friend Amber Cheeseman?'

My blood literally ran cold, and I froze in front of the G and T room, my phone clutched to my face.

'W-what?'

'I wonder what Amber would say,' Grandmere went on, 'if I happened to mention to her how you'd squandered the money for her commencement ceremony on recycling bins.'

I was too shocked to speak. I just stood there, while

Boris tried to edge past me with his violin case, going, 'Um, excuse me, Mia.'

'Grandmere,' I said, barely able to speak because my throat had gone so dry. 'You wouldn't.'

Her reply rocked me to my very core:

'Oh, I would.'

GRANDMERE, I wanted to scream. YOU CAN'T GO AROUND THREATENING YOUR ONLY GRANDDAUGHTER!!!!!!!!!!! WHAT IS WRONG WITH YOU??????

But of course I couldn't. Scream that. Because I was in the middle of the Gifted and Talented room. On a cellphone.

And even if it IS Gifted and Talented, and everyone in that class is incredibly weird anyway, you can't go around screaming into cellphones there.

'I thought that might change your outlook on the situation,' Grandmere purred. 'I will, of course, say nothing to your little friend about the state of the class treasury. But, in return, you will help solve my current real-estate crisis by starring in *Braid!*. The fact is, Amelia, as an ancestress of Rosagunde, you will lend much more authenticity to the role than your friend Lilly would – besides which, you are much more attractive than Lilly, who, in certain lights, often resembles one of those dogs with the flat faces.'

A pug! And I thought I was the only one who'd ever noticed!

'See you at rehearsal tonight, Amelia,' Grandmere sang. 'Oh, and, if you know what's good for you, young lady, you'll mention our little agreement – particularly the part about the *incentive* I've provided to make your participation worth your while – to no one. NO ONE, including your father. Understand?'

Then she hung up.

!!!!!!!!!!!!!!!!!!!!

I can't believe this. I really can't. I mean, I guess I always secretly kind of knew it, deep down inside. But she's never done anything quite this BLATANT before.

Still, I guess I finally have to admit it, since it really is true:

My grandmother is EVIL. Seriously.

Because what kind of woman uses BLACKMAIL to get her granddaughter to do her bidding?

I'll tell you what kind: an EVIL one.

Or possibly Grandmere's a sociopath. It wouldn't surprise me in the least. She exhibits all the major symptoms. Except possibly the one about breaking laws repeatedly.

But while Grandmere may not break *federal* laws, she breaks laws of common decency ALL the time.

After I'd hung up with Grandmere, I caught Lilly staring at me over the computer on which she was doing the layout for the first issue of *Fat Louie's Pink Butthole*.

'Something wrong, Mia?' she wanted to know.

'About the Rosagunde thing,' I explained to her. 'I'm sorry, but Grandmere won't budge. She says I have to play her, or she'll tell You Know Who about You Know What and I'll get my butt kicked from here to Westchester.'

Lilly's dark eyes glittered behind her glasses. 'Oh, she did, did she?' She doesn't look surprised.

'I really am sorry, Lilly,' I said, meaning it. 'You would have made a way better Rosagunde than me.'

'Whatever,' Lilly said with a sniff. 'I'll be fine with my part. Really.'

I could tell she just being brave, though. Inside, she's really hurting.

And I don't blame her. None of it makes any sense. If Grandmere wants her show to be a success, why wouldn't she want the best actress she could find? Why would she insist on the part being played by ME, basically the worst actress in the whole school – with the possible exception of Amber Cheeseman?

Oh, well. Who knows why Grandmere does half the things she does? I imagine there's some kind of rationale to it.

But we mere humans will never understand what it is. That is a privilege reserved only for the other aliens from the mother ship that brought my grandmother here from the evil planet she was born on.

Friday, March 5, Earth Science

Just now Kenny asked me if I would re-copy our mole-mass worksheet, because last night, while completing it, he got Szechuan sauce on it.

I don't know what got into me. Maybe it was residual meanness left over from my conversation with Grandmere. I mean, like, maybe some of HER meanness rubbed off on me, or something. I don't know of any other way to explain it.

In any case, whatever it was, I decided to employ economic theory to the situation. I just thought, Why not? The whole self-actualization thing hasn't worked out for me. Why not give old Alfred Marshall a try? Everyone else seems to be doing it. Like Lana.

And SHE always gets what SHE wants. Just like GRANDMERE always gets what SHE wants.

So I told Kenny I wouldn't do it unless he did tonight's homework too.

He looked at me kind of funny, but he said he would. I guess he looked at me funny because he does our homework EVERY night.

Still. I can't believe it has taken me this long to catch on to how society works. All this time, I thought it was Jungian transcendence I needed in order to find serenity and contentment.

But Grandmere – and Lana Weinberger, of all people – have shown me the error of my ways.

It's not about forming a base of roots such as trust and compassion in order to reap the fruits of joy and love.

No. It's about the laws of supply and demand. If you

demand something, and can provide a proper incentive to get people to hand it over, they'll *supply* it.

And the equilibrium remains stable.

It's sort of amazing. I had no idea Grandmere was such an economic genius.

Or that LANA would ever teach ME something.

It sort of casts everything in a new light.

And I do mean *everything*.

Homework:
Homeroom: N/A
PE: GYM SHORTS!!! GYM SHORTS!!!! GYM SHORTS!!!!!
US Economics: read Chapter 9 for Monday
English: pages 155–175, *O Pioneers!*
French: vocabulaire 3ème étape
G and T: find that water bra Lilly bought me that time as a joke. Wear it to the party
Geometry: Chapter 18
Earth Science: who cares? Kenny's doing it! Ha HA HA HA

Friday, March 5, the Ballroom at the Plaza

For the first rehearsal ever of *Braid!* we had what Grandmere called a 'read-through'. We were supposed to read the script together as a group, each actor saying his or her lines out loud, the way he or she would if we were performing the show on stage.

Can I just say read-throughs are very boring?

I had my journal tucked up behind my script so no one could see that I was writing instead of following along. Although it was kind of awkward to shift the script out from behind my journal when one of my cues came up.

A cue is the line before you are supposed to say yours. I am finding out all sorts of theatry stuff today.

Like, Grandmere, while she may have written the dialogue for *Braid!*, she didn't write the MUSIC. The music was composed by this guy named Phil. Phil is the same guy who was playing the piano to accompany us at the audition yesterday. Grandmere, it turns out, paid Phil a ton of money to write music to go with her lyrics for all the songs in *Braid!*.

She says she got his name off the employment board at Hunter College.

Phil doesn't look like he's had much time to enjoy his new-found cash windfall, though. Basically, he pulled an all-nighter to compose the music for *Braid!*, and it looks as if he still hasn't really caught up with his sleep. He seemed to be having a lot of trouble staying awake during the read-through.

He wasn't the only one. Señor Eduardo didn't open his eyes ONCE after the play's first line (uttered by Rosagunde: 'Oh, la, what a joy it is to live in this sleepy,

auditioned for every single show the AEHS drama
has ever put on is because his mom and dad are
the theatre, and always wanted to have a
Business.

'But I'd rather write for a living,' J.P
know, that there are a lot of jobs out t
I mean, I'd rather be a writer th
actors, when you think about it
pret stuff somebody else h
POWER. The real power'
which someone else ha
ested in. Being the p
Jude Laws of this

This is so
same thin

Plus
do s
p

except, you know, he's not a royal.

Still, I was talking to him a little bit before rehearsal started (because I saw that everyone else was ignoring him – well, Boris and Tina were busy making out, as they do much more now that Boris no longer wears a bionater, and Lilly was going over her editorial remarks about Kenny's dwarf-star thesis with him, and Perin was trying to convince Grandmere that she's a girl, not a guy, and Ling Su was trying to keep Amber Cheeseman away from me, as she has promised she will do in her capacity as chorus member) and J.P. told me that he has no real interest in acting – that the only reason he has

club
nuts for
son in the

. said. 'Not, you
here for poets. But
an an actor. Because
their job is just to inter-
as written. They have no
s in the words they're saying,
written. That's what I'm inter-
ower *behind* the Julia Robertses and
world.'

freaky!!!! Because I said almost the exact
g once!!!! I think.

I understand what it feels like, that pressure to
omething just to make your parents happy. Case in
oint: Princess lessons. Oh, and not flunking Geometry
even though it will do me no earthly good in my future.

The only problem is, even though he's tried out for all
the shows AEHS has put on, J.P.'s never got a single part.
He thinks the reason is because of the Drama Club's
cliquishness.

'I mean, I guess if I REALLY wanted a part in one of
their shows,' he told me, 'I could have started trying to
get in with their group – you know, sit with them at
lunch, hang out with them on the steps before school,
fetch coffee from Ho's for them, get my nose pierced,
start smoking clove cigarettes, and all that. But the
truth is, I really can't stand actors. They're so self-
absorbed! I just get tired of being the audience for their
performance pieces, you know? Because that's basically

what it's like when you talk to one. Like they're doing a monologue just for you.'

'Well,' I said, thinking of all the stories I'd read about teen actors in *Us Weekly*. 'Maybe that's because they're insecure. Most teens are, you know. Insecure, I mean.'

I didn't mention that, of all the teens J.P. had ever spoken to, I am probably the one who is the MOST insecure. Not that I don't have good reason to be insecure. I mean, how many other teens do you know who have no earthly clue how to party and who have grandmas who try to blackmail them?

'Maybe,' J.P. said. 'Or maybe I'm just too critical. The truth is, I don't think I'm really the club-joining type. I'm sort of more of a loner. In case you didn't notice.'

J.P. grinned at me after he said that, a sort of sheepish grin. I could sort of start to see what Tina and Lilly were saying, about him being cute. He IS sort of cute. In a big, teddy-bearish sort of way.

And he's right about actors. I mean, judging by what I've seen of them on talk shows. They never shut up about themselves!

And OK, I guess the interviewer is asking. But still.

Oops, my turn again:

'Handmaid, fetch me the strongest grappa from the storerooms! I shall teach this rogue what it means to trifle with the house of Renaldo.'

Oh, God. Two hours until I get to see Michael. I have never needed to smell his neck more than I do now. Of course I can't tell him what's bothering me – the whole thing about my being such a non-party girl – but at least I can find some comfort standing next to him in his parents' kitchen as I make dip, listening to the rumble of

161

his deep voice as he tells me about chaos theory, or whatever.

PLEASE MAKE THIS END.

Oops, my turn again:

'In the name of my father, I dispatch you, Lord Alboin, to hell, where you belong!'

Yay! Joy and felicitations! Alboin is dead! Sing the closing song, then circle round for the finale! Yippee! We can all go home now! Or out on our dates!

No, wait. Grandmere has one last announcement:

'I'd like to thank you all for agreeing to join me on the extraordinary journey we are about to make together. Rehearsing and putting on *Braid!* should be one of the most creatively fulfilling projects any of you have ever attempted. And I think the rewards will be far more than we ever imagined we'd reap –'

Nice of her to look right at me as she says this last part. Why doesn't she just come right out and say, *And Amber Cheeseman won't kill you for losing all the commencement money.*

'But before we can come close to achieving those rewards, we are going to need to work, and work hard,' she went on. 'Rehearsals will be daily and will last late into the night. And you will, of course, have your lines completely memorized by Monday.'

Her statement caused even more trepidatious murmuring. Rommel, disturbed by the obvious psychic pain in the room, started licking his nether regions compulsively, as he does during times of duress.

'I don't think I can learn all the Italian words I have to know by then, Your Highness,' Perin said nervously.

'Nonsense,' Grandmere said. '*Nessun dolore, nessun guadagno.*'

But since nobody even knew what that meant, they were still freaking out.

Except J.P., apparently. He said, in his deep, calm, *My Bodyguard* voice, 'Hey, guys, come on. I think we can do this. It'll be kind of fun.'

It took a second or two for this to sink in. But when it finally did, it was Lilly, surprisingly, who said, 'You know, J.P.'s right. I think we can do it too.'

Which caused Boris to burst out with, 'Excuse me, but weren't you the one who was just complaining about how you have the first issue of the school's new literary magazine to put to bed this weekend?'

Lilly chose to ignore that. J.P. looked kind of confused.

'Well, I don't know about putting magazines to bed,' he said. 'But I bet if we get together tomorrow morning, and maybe Sunday too, and do a few more read-throughs, we'll have most of our lines memorized by Monday.'

'Excellent idea,' Grandmere said, clapping her hands loudly enough to cause Señor Eduardo to open his eyes groggily. 'That will give us plenty of time to work with the choreographer and vocal instructor.'

'Choreographer?' Boris looked horrified. 'Vocal instructor? Just how much time are we talking about here?'

'As much time,' Grandmere said fiercely, 'as it takes. Now, all of you go home and get some rest! I suggest eating a hearty supper to give you strength for tomorrow's rehearsal. A steak, cooked medium rare, with a small salad and a baked potato with plenty of butter and salt is the ideal repast for a thespian who wants to keep up his or her strength. I will expect to see all of you here tomorrow morning at ten. And eat a big breakfast – eggs and bacon, and plenty of coffee! I don't want any of my actors fainting from exhaustion on me! And good read-through, people! Excellent! You showed plenty of good, raw emotion. Give yourselves a round of applause!'

Slowly, one by one, we started to clap – only because, if we didn't, it was clear Grandmere was never going to let us out of there.

Unfortunately, our applause woke the dozing maestro. Or director. Or whatever he was.

'Tank you!' Señor Eduardo was now awake enough to think that we were clapping for something he did. 'Tank you, all! I could not have done eet eef eet were not for you, however. You are all too kind.'

'Well.' J.P. waved to me. 'See you tomorrow morning, Mia. Don't forget to eat that steak! And that bacon!'

'She's a vegetarian,' Boris, who still seemed sort of hostile about how much violin practice he was going to miss, reminded him.

J.P. blinked.

'I know,' he said. 'That was a joke. I mean, after she freaked out about the meat in the vegetarian lasagne that one time, the whole SCHOOL knows she's a vegetarian.'

'Oh yeah?' Boris said. 'Well, you're one to talk, Mr Guy Who Hates It When They—'

I had to slap my hand over Boris's mouth before he could finish.

'Good night, J.P.,' I said. 'See you tomorrow!' Then, after he'd left the room, I let Boris go, and had to wipe my hand on a napkin.

'God, Boris,' I said. 'Drool much?'

'I have a problem with over-secretion of saliva,' he informed me.

164

'NOW you tell me.'

'Wow, Mia,' Lilly said, as we were on our way out. 'Way to overreact. What is wrong with you anyway? Do you *like* that J.P. guy or something?'

'No,' I said, offended. Jeez, I mean, I've only been dating her brother for nearly a year and a half. She should KNOW by now who I like. 'But you guys could at least be nice to him.'

'Mia just feels guilty,' Boris observed, 'because she killed him off in her short story.'

'No, I don't,' I snapped.

But as usual, I was fully lying. I *do* feel guilty about killing J.P. in my story.

And I hereby swear I will never kill another character based on a real person in my fiction again.

Except when I write my book about Grandmere of course.

Friday, March 5, 10 p.m., the Moscovitzes' living room

OK, these movies Michael is making me watch? They are so depressing! Dystopic science fiction just isn't my thing. I mean, even the WORD dystopic bums me out. Because dystopia is the OPPOSITE of utopia, which means an idyllic or totally peaceful society. Like the utopian society they tried to build in New Harmony, Indiana, where my mom made me go one time when we were trying to get away from Mamaw and Papaw during a visit to Versailles (the one in Indiana).

In New Harmony, everyone got together and planned this like perfect city with all these pretty buildings and pretty streets and pretty schools and stuff. I know it sounds repulsive. But it's not. New Harmony is actually cool.

A dystopic society, on the other hand, is NOT cool. There are no pretty buildings or streets or schools. It's a lot like the Lower East Side used to be before all the rich dot com geniuses moved down there and they opened all those tapas bars and $3,000-a-month maintenance-fee condos, actually. You know, one of those places where everything is pretty much gas stations and strip clubs, with the occasional crack dealer on the corner thrown in for good measure.

Which is the kind of society heroes in pretty much all the dystopic sci-fi movies we've seen tonight have lived in.

The Omega Man? Dystopic society brought on by mass plague that killed most of the population and left everybody (except Charlton Heston) a zombie.

Logan's Run? Utopian society that turns out to be dystopic when it is revealed that in order to feed the population with the limited resources left to them after a nuclear holocaust, the government is forced to disintegrate its citizens on their thirtieth birthdays.

2001: A Space Odyssey is up next, at least as soon as I get out of the bathroom, but I seriously don't think I can take it any more.

The only thing making any of this bearable is that I get to snuggle up next to Michael on the couch.

And that we get to make out during the slow parts.

And that during the scary parts, I get to bury my head against his chest and he wraps his arms around me all tight and I get to smell his neck.

And while this would be more than satisfying under normal circumstances, there is the small fact that whenever things start getting REALLY passionate between Michael and me – like, heated enough for him to actually press pause on the remote – we can hear Lilly down the hall screaming, 'A curse upon you, Alboin, for the scurrilous dog I always knew you to be!'

Can I just say it's very hard to get swept away in the arms of your one true love when you can hear someone yelling, 'You would take this common Genovian wench to wed when you could have me, Alboin? Fie!'

Which may be why Michael just went to the kitchen to get us some more popcorn. It looks like *2001: A Space Odyssey* may be our only hope for drowning out Lilly's not-so-dulcet tones as she and Lars rehearse her lines.

Although – seeing as how I'm making this new effort to stop lying so much – I should probably admit that it's not just Lilly's strident rehearsing that's keeping me from being able to give Michael my full attention, make-out-wise. The truth is, this party thing is weighing down on me like that banana snake Britney wore at the VMAs that one time.

It's killing me inside. It really is. I mean, I made the dip – French onion, you know, from the Knorr's pack – and everything, to make him think I'm looking forward to tomorrow night and all.

But I'm so not.

At least I have a plan, though. Thanks to Lana. About what I'm going to do during the party. I mean, the dancing thing. And I have an outfit. Well, sort of. I think I might have cut my skirt a little TOO short.

Although to Lana, there's probably no such thing.

Oooooh, Michael's back, with more popcorn. Kissing time!

Saturday, March 6, midnight

Close call: when I got home from the Moscovitzes this evening, my mom was waiting up for me (well, not exactly waiting up for ME. She was watching that three-part *Extreme Surgery* on Discovery Health about the guy with the enormous facial birthmark that even eight surgeries couldn't totally get rid of. And he couldn't even put a mask on that side of his face like the *Phantom of the Opera* guy, because his birthmark was all bumpy and stuck out too far for any mask to fit over. And Christine would just be all, *Um, I can totally see your scars even with your mask, dude.* Plus he probably didn't have an underground grotto to take her to anyway. But whatever).

Even though I tried to sneak in all quietly, Mom caught me, and we had to have the conversation I'd really been hoping to avoid:

Mom (putting the TV on mute):	Mia, what is this I hear about your grandmother putting on some kind of musical about your ancestress Rosagunde and casting you in the lead?
Me:	Um. Yeah. About that.
Mom:	That is the most ridiculous thing I have ever heard. Doesn't she realize you are barely passing Geometry? You don't have time to be starring in any play. You have to concentrate on your studies. You have enough

extra-curricular activities, what with the president thing and princess lessons. And now this? Who does she think she's kidding?

Me: Musical.

Mom: What?

Me: It's a musical, not a play.

Mom: I don't care what it is. I'm calling your father tomorrow and telling him to make her cut it out.

Me (stricken,   No! Don't! Please, Mom? I
because if she does   really . . . um . . . I really love it.
that, Grandmere
will totally spill the
beans to Amber
Cheeseman about
the money, and I will
be elbowed in the
throat. But I can't
tell Mom that either,
so I have to lie.
Again):

Mom: Love what?

Me: The play. I mean, musical. I

170

	really want to do it. Theatre is my life. Please don't make me stop.
Mom:	Mia. Are you feeling all right?
Me:	Fine! Just don't call Dad, OK? He's really busy with Parliament and everything right now. Let's not bother him. I really like Grandmere's play. It's fun and a good chance for me to, um, broaden my horizons.
Mom:	Well . . . I don't know . . .
Me:	Please, Mom. I swear my grades won't slip.
Mom:	Well. All right. But if you bring home so much as a single C on a quiz, I'm calling Genovia.
Me:	Oh, thanks, Mom! Don't worry, I won't.

Then I had to go into my room and breathe into a paper bag, because I thought I might be hyperventilating.

Saturday, March 6, 2 p.m., Ballroom at the Plaza

OK, so acting may be a little harder than I thought it was. I mean, that thing I wrote a while back, about how the reason so many people want to be actors is because it's really easy and you get paid a lot . . .

That might be true. But it turns out it's not that easy. There's a whole lot of stuff you have to remember.

Like blocking. That's like where you move on the stage as you're saying your lines. I always thought actors just got to make this up as they go along.

But it turns out the director tells them exactly where to move, and even on which word in which line to do it. And how fast. And in which direction.

At least, if that director is Grandmere.

Not that she's the director, of course. Or so she keeps assuring us. Señor Eduardo, propped up in a corner with a blanket covering him to his chin, is REALLY directing this play. I mean, musical.

But, since he can barely stay awake long enough to say, 'And . . . scene!', Grandmere has generously come forward to take over.

I'm not saying this wasn't her plan all along. But she sure isn't admitting it if it was.

Anyway, in addition to all our lines, we also have to remember our blocking.

Blocking isn't choreography, though. Choreography is the dancing you do while you're singing the songs.

For this, Grandmere hired a professional choreographer. Her name is Feather. Feather is apparently very famous for choreographing several hit Broadway shows. She also must be pretty hard up for cash if she'd agree to choreograph a snoozer like *Braid!* But whatever.

Feather is nothing like the choreographers I've seen in dancing movies like *Honey* or *Center Stage*. She doesn't wear any make-up, says her leotard was made from hemp, and she keeps asking us to find our centres and focus on our chi.

When Feather says things like this, Grandmere looks annoyed. But I know she doesn't want to yell at Feather since she'd be hard-pressed to find a new choreographer at such short notice if Feather quits in a fit of pique, as dancers are apparently prone to do.

But Feather isn't as bad as the vocal coach, Madame Puissant, who normally works with opera singers at the Met and who made us all stand there and do vocal exercises, or *vocalastics*, as she called it, which involved singing the words *Me, May, Ma, Mo, Moooo-oooo-oooo-ooo* over and over again in ever-increasing pitches until we could 'feel the tingle in the bridge of our nose'.

Madame Puissant clearly doesn't care about the state of our chis because she noticed Lilly wasn't wearing any fingernail polish and almost sent her home because 'a diva never goes anywhere with bare nails'.

I noticed Grandmere seems to approve VERY highly of Madame Puissant. At least, she doesn't interrupt her at all, the way she does Feather.

As if all of this was not enough, there were also costume measurements to endure, and, in my case anyway, wig-fittings as well. Because of course the character of Rosagunde has to have this enormously long braid, since that is, after all, the title of the play.

I mean, musical.

I'm just saying, everyone was worried about getting their LINES memorized in time, but it turns out there is WAY more involved in putting on a play – I mean, musical – than just memorizing your lines. You have to know your blocking and choreography as well, not to mention all the songs and how not to trip over your braid, which, since we don't have a braid yet, in my case means not tripping over one of those velvet ropes they used to drape outside the Palm Court to keep people from storming it before it opened for afternoon tea, and which Grandmere has wrapped around my head.

I guess it isn't any wonder I have a little headache. Although it's not any worse than the ones I get every time they cram me into a tiara.

Right now J.P. and I have a little break because Feather is going over the choreography for the chorus of the song 'Genovia!' which everyone but he and I sing. It turns out that Kenny, in addition to not being able to sing or act, can't dance either, so it is taking a really long time.

That's OK, though, because I'm using the time to plot tonight's Party Strategy and talk to J.P., who really turns out to know a LOT about the theatre. That's on account of his father being a famous producer. J.P. has been hanging around the stage since he was a little kid, and he's met tons of celebrities because of it.

'John Travolta, Antonio Banderas, Bruce Willis, Renée Zellweger, Julia Roberts . . . pretty much everybody there is to meet,' is how J.P. replied, when I asked him who he meant by celebrities.

Wow. I bet Tina would change places with J.P. in a New York minute, even if it meant, you know. Becoming a boy.

I asked J.P. if there was any celebrity he HADN'T met that he wanted to, and he said just one: David Mamet, the famous playwright.

'You know,' he said. *'Glengarry Glen Ross. About Last Night . . . Oleanna.'*

'Oh, sure,' I said, like I knew what he was talking about.

I told him that was still pretty impressive – I mean, that he'd met almost everybody else in Hollywood.

'Yeah,' he said. 'But you know, when it comes down to it, celebrities are just people, like you and me. Well, I mean, like me, anyway. You – well, you're a celebrity. You must get that a lot. You know, people thinking you're – I don't know. This one thing. When really, you're not. That's just the public's perception of you. That must be really hard.'

Were truer words ever spoken? I mean, look at what I'm dealing with right now: this perception that I'm not a party girl. When I most certainly AM. I mean, I'm going to a party tonight, right?

And OK, I'm totally dreading it and had to ask advice about it from the meanest girl in my whole school.

But that doesn't mean I'm not a party girl.

Anyway, in addition to having met every single celebrity in the world except David Mamet, J.P. has been to every single play ever put on, including – and I couldn't believe this – *Beauty and the Beast*.

And get this: It's one of his all-time favourites too.

I can't believe that for all this time, I've been seeing him as the Guy Who Hates It When They Put Corn In The Chilli – you know, just this freak in the cafeteria – when underneath, he's like this really cool, funny guy who writes poems about Principal Gupta and likes *Beauty and the Beast* and would like to meet David Mamet (whoever that is).

But I guess that's just a reflection of how the

educational system today, being so overcrowded and impersonal, makes it so hard for adolescents to break through our preconceived notions of one another and get to know the real person underneath the label they're given, be it Princess, Brainiac, Drama Geek, Jock, Cheerleader or Guy Who Hates It When They Put Corn In The Chilli.

Oops. Chorus rehearsal is over. Grandmere's calling for the Principal Characters now.

Which means J.P and me. We sure have a lot of scenes together. Especially seeing as how up until I read *Braid!*, I never even knew my ancestress Rosagunde HAD a boyfriend.

Saturday, March 6, 6 p.m., Limo on the way home from the Plaza

Oh my God, I'm soooo tired, I can barely keep my eyes open. Acting is SO HARD. Who knew? I mean, those kids on *Degrassi* make it look so easy. But they're going to school and everything the whole time they're filming that show. How do they DO it?

Of course, they don't have to sing, except for those episodes where there's like a band audition or whatever. Singing is even harder than ACTING, it turns out. And I thought that was the thing I'd have the least trouble with, because of my intensive self-training in the event I have to perform karaoke on a road trip to make food money like Britney in *Crossroads*.

Well, let me just say that I have a new-found respect for Kelis because to get that one perfect version of 'Milkshake' on her album, she had to have rehearsed it five thousand times. Madame Puissant made me rehearse 'Rosagunde's Song' at LEAST that many times.

And when my voice started to get scratchy and I couldn't hit the high notes, she made me grab the bottom of the baby grand piano Phil was accompanying me on, and LIFT!

'Sing from the diaphragm, *Princesse*,' was what Madame Puissant kept yelling. 'No breathing from the chest. From the DIAPHRAGM! No chest voice! SING FROM THE DIAPHRAGM! LIFT!!! LIFT!!!!'

I was just glad I'd put clear polish on all my nails the other day (so I'd be less tempted to bite them). At least she couldn't yell at me about THAT.

And choreography? Forget about it. Some people look down on cheerleaders (OK, me included, except for Shameeka – up until now), but that stuff is HARD!!! Remembering all those steps??? Oh my God! It's like, 'Take my chi already, Feather! I can't step-ball-change any more!'

But Feather didn't have the least bit of sympathy for me – and she had even LESS for Kenny, who can't step-ball-change to save his life.

And guess what? We're all expected to show up at ten tomorrow morning for more of the same.

Boris said tonight, as we were all leaving, 'This is the hardest I have ever had to work for a hundred extra credit points.'

Which is a totally good point. But, as Ling Su mentioned to him, it beats selling candles door-to-door.

After which I had to shush her, because Amber Cheeseman had been standing nearby!

Except of course J.P. overheard me shushing Ling Su, and was like, 'What? What's the big secret? What are you guys talking about? You can tell me, I swear I'll take it to the grave.'

The thing is, when you are thrown together for so many hours, the way we've all been since rehearsals started, you sort of . . . bond. I mean, you can't help it. You're just in each other's company SO MUCH. Even Lilly, who has markedly anti-social tendencies, yelled, as we were all putting on our coats, 'Hey, you guys, I almost forgot! Party tonight at my place! You should totally come, my parents are out of town!'

Which I thought was kind of bold of her – it's Michael's party, really, not hers, and I don't know how thrilled he'll be if a bunch of high-school kids show up (besides me, of course).

But, you know. It's an example of how close we all feel to one another.

And also why I felt forced to tell J.P. the truth – that the student government had run a little short of cash to pay for the seniors' commencement ceremony, and that was why we were putting on *Braid!* in the first place.

J.P. seemed surprised to hear this – but not, as I first thought, because he was shocked to learn I'd messed up the budget.

'Really?' he said. 'And here I was thinking that this whole thing was just an elaborate ruse by your grand-mother to sucker my dad into giving up his bid on the faux island of Genovia.'

!!!!!!!!!!!!!!!!!!!!!!!!!!!!!!!!!

I just stared at him with my mouth hanging open until he laughed and said, 'Mia, don't worry. I won't tell. About the money for commencement OR your grand-mother's scheme.'

But then I got all curious, and was like, 'Why does your dad want to buy the faux island of Genovia anyway, J.P.?'

'Because he can,' J.P. said, not looking jokey at all – which, for him, was a first. He almost never seems to look upset or worried about anything – except corn of course.

I could see right away that John Paul Reynolds-Abernathy the Third was a sore subject to John Paul Reynolds-Abernathy the Fourth. So I dropped it. That's the kind of thing you learn when you're training to be a princess. How to drop subjects that suddenly seem to turn uncomfortable.

'Well, see you tomorrow,' I said to J.P..

'Are you going to Lilly's party?' he wanted to know.

'Oh,' I said. 'Yes.'

'Maybe I'll see you there then,' J.P. said.

Which is sweet. You know, that J.P. feels comfortable enough with us to want to come to Lilly's party. Even if he doesn't know it's Michael's party, and not Lilly's.

Anyway, I've got more important things to worry about right now than J.P. and Lilly and Grandmere and her diabolical schemes for faux-island domination.

Because I've got a scheme of my own to put into action . . .

Sunday, March 7, 1 a.m., the Loft

I'm so embarrassed. Seriously. I'm MORTIFIED. This is probably the most embarrassed I have ever been in my entire life.

And I know I've said that before, but this time I really mean it.

I really thought, for a while there, that it might have been working. My plan to prove to Michael that I really am a party girl, I mean.

I don't understand exactly what went wrong. I had it ALL planned out. I did EXACTLY what Lana said. As soon as I got to Lilly and Michael's apartment, I changed out of my rehearsal clothes into my party clothes:

- Black tights
- My black velvet skirt (transformed into a mini – the edges were kind of raggedy because Fat Louie kept batting at the scissors as I was cutting, but what-ever, it still looked OK)
- My black Docs
- A black leotard left over from that Halloween I dressed as a cat and Ronnie from next door said I looked like a flat-chested *Playboy* bunny so I never wore it again
- A black beret my mom used to wear when she was performing acts of civil disobedience with her fel-low Guerilla Girls
- And the water bra. Which I didn't even fill up all that much, because, you know, I was scared of leaks.

Plus I put on red lipstick and tousled my hair all sexily, like Lindsay Lohan's when she's coming out of

New York clubs like Butter after just narrowly having missed running into her ex, Wilmer.

But instead of being all, 'That's hot,' about my new look, Michael – who was answering the door as the first of his guests began to arrive, just raised his eyebrows at me like he was kind of alarmed about something.

And Lars actually looked up from his Sidekick as I walked by and started to say something, but then apparently thought better of it, since he went back to leaning against the wall and looking up stuff on the Web.

And then Lilly, who was busy getting her camera ready to film the festivities for a piece she's doing for *Lilly Tells It Like Is* on male–female dynamics in a modern urban setting, was like, 'What are you supposed to be? A mime?'

But instead of getting mad at her, I tossed my head, the way Lana does, and was like, 'Aren't you funny?'

Because I was trying to act mature in front of Michael's friends, who were coming in just then.

And I guess I succeeded, because Trevor and Felix were like, 'Mia?' as if they didn't recognize me. Even Paul was all, 'Nice sticks,' which I guess was a compliment about my legs, which look quite long when I wear a short skirt.

Even Doo Pak went, 'Oh, Princess Mia, you are looking very nice without your overalls.'

And J.P. – who showed up a little while later, at the same time as Tina and Boris – said, '"Your beauty would put even the loveliest Mediterranean sunset to shame, my lady,"' which is one of his lines from the play, but whatever, it was still nice.

And he accompanied it with the same courtly bow from the play too. I mean, musical.

Michael was the only one who didn't say anything. But I figured it was because he was too busy putting on the music and making everyone feel at home. Also, he wasn't too thrilled Lilly had invited Boris and those guys without asking him first.

So I tried to help him out. You know, make things go smoother. I went up to some girls from his dorm who had come in – none of whom was wearing a beret or even a particularly sexy outfit. Unless you consider Tevas with socks sexy – and was like, 'Hi, I'm Michael's girlfriend, Mia. Would you like some dip?'

I didn't mention that I'd made the dip myself, because I didn't think a true party girl would really make her own dip. Like, I doubt Lana's ever made dip. Making dip was a bad miscalculation on my part, but not one that was impossible to overcome, because I didn't have to *tell* people I'd made the dip.

The college girls said they didn't want any dip, even when I assured them I had made it with low-fat mayonnaise and sour cream. Because I know college girls are always watching their weight in order to avoid gaining that Freshman Fifteen. Although I didn't SAY this to them, of course.

But I wasn't going to let their refusal of dip get me down. I mean, that had really just been an opening to start a conversation with them.

Only they didn't seem to really want to talk to me very much. And Boris and Tina were making out on the couch, and Lilly was showing J.P. how her camera worked. So I didn't have anyone to talk to.

So I sort of drifted over to the kitchen and got a beer. I figured this is what a party girl would do. Because Lana had told me so. I took the cap off with the bottle opener that was lying there, and since I saw that everyone else was drinking their beer straight out of the bottle, I did the same.

And nearly gagged. Because beer tasted even worse than I remembered. Like worse than that skunk Papaw ran over smelt.

But since no one else was making a face every time they drank from their beer bottle, I tried to control myself and settled for taking very small sips. That made it a little more bearable. Maybe that's how beer drinkers stand it. By taking in very small amounts of it at a time. I kept on taking small sips until I noticed J.P. had Lilly's camera and was pointing it right at me. At which point I hid the beer behind my back.

J.P. lowered the camera. He said, 'Sorry,' and looked really uncomfortable.

But not as uncomfortable as I felt, when Lilly, who was standing next to him, went, 'Mia. What are you doing?'

'Nothing,' I said to her in an annoyed voice. Because that is how I imagined a party girl would feel about her friend asking her what she was doing. Unless she was one of those party girls from *Girls Gone Wild*, in which case she'd just have lifted up her shirt for the camera.

But I decided I wasn't that kind of party girl.

'You're drinking?' Lilly looked sort of shocked. Well, maybe more amused than shocked, actually. *'Beer?'*

'I'm just trying to have a good time,' I said. I was excruciatingly aware of J.P.'s gaze on me. Why that should have made me feel so uncomfortable, I don't know. It just did. 'It's not like I don't drink all the time in Genovia.'

'Sure,' Lilly said. 'Champagne toasts with foreign dignitaries. Wine with dinner. Not *beer*.'

'Whatever,' I said, again. And moved away from her – – and smacked right into Michael, who was like, 'Oh, hey, there you are.'

And then he looked down at the beer in my hand and went, 'What are you doing?'

'Oh, you know,' I said, tossing my head again, all casual and party-girl-like. 'Just having a good time.'

'Since when do you drink beer?' Michael wanted to know.

'God, Michael,' I said, laughing. 'Whatever.'

'She said the same thing to me,' Lilly informed her brother, as she took her camera from J.P. and stuck the lens into both our faces.

'Lilly,' Michael said. 'Quit filming. Mia—'

But before he got to say whatever it was he was going to say, his computer's Party Shuffle (he'd wired the speakers in his parents' living room to his hard drive) started to play the first slowish song of the evening – Coldplay's 'Speed of Sound' – so I went, 'Oh, I love this song,' and started dancing, the way Lana had said to.

The truth is, I am not even the biggest Coldplay fan, because I don't really approve of the lead singer letting his wife, Gwyneth Paltrow, name their kid Apple. What is going to happen to that poor kid when she gets to high school? Everyone is going to make fun of her.

But I guess that beer, skunky as it had been, did the trick. Because I didn't feel anywhere near as self-conscious as I had before I'd started sipping it. In fact, I felt sort of good. Even though I was the only person in the whole room who was dancing.

But I figured that was OK because a lot of times

185

when one person starts dancing, everyone else will. They are just waiting for someone to break the ice.

Only I couldn't help noticing as I danced, that no one was joining me. Especially Michael. He was just standing there staring at me. As was Lars. As was Lilly, although she was doing it through a camera lens. Boris and Tina, over on the couch, stopped kissing and started looking at me instead. Also, the college girls were staring at me too. One of them leaned over to whisper something to one of her friends, and the friend giggled.

I figured they were just jealous because I had actually made an effort to dress up for the party, what with my beret and all, and kept dancing.

Which was when J.P. totally came to my rescue. He started dancing too.

He wasn't really dancing *with* me, since he wasn't touching me, or anything. But he kind of walked over to where I was and started moving his feet around, you know, the way really big guys dance, like they don't want to draw a lot of attention to themselves, but they want to join in the fun.

I was so excited someone else was finally dancing, I sort of shimmied (Feather taught us that term – it's when you wiggle your shoulders) closer to him, and smiled up at him, to say thanks. And he smiled back.

The thing is, after that, I guess – technically speaking – we *were* sort of dancing together. I guess, technically, what was happening was, I was dancing with another guy. In front of my boyfriend. At a party being *given* by my boyfriend.

Which I guess – technically speaking – constitutes really bad girlfriend behaviour.

Although I didn't realize it at the time. At the time,

all I could think about was how stupid I'd felt when no one would dance with me, and how happy I was that J.P. – unlike my other so-called friends – hadn't left me hanging there, dancing by myself, in front of everyone . . . particularly Michael.

Who hadn't even told me I looked nice. Or that he liked my beret.

J.P. had said I looked more beautiful than the loveliest Mediterranean sunset. *J.P.* had come over and started dancing with me.

While Michael just stood there.

Who knew how long J.P. and I would have kept dancing – while Michael just stood there – if right then the front door hadn't opened, and Dr and Dr Moscovitz hadn't come in?

And OK, Michael had got permission to have the party and they weren't mad about it at all.

But still! They walked in right as I was dancing! With ANOTHER GUY! It was super embarrassing!!! I mean, they're Michael's PARENTS!!!!

This was almost as embarrassing as the time they walked in when Michael and I were kissing, you know, on the couch over Winter Break (well, OK, we were doing MORE than kissing. There was some under-the-shirt and over-the-bra action going on. Which I will admit for a girl who doesn't want to have sex until prom of her senior year is pretty risky behaviour. But whatever. The truth is, I got so involved in the whole kissing thing, I didn't even notice what Michael's hands were doing until it was too late. Because by then I was LIKING it. So in a way, I was like, THANK GOD Dr and Dr Moscovitz walked in when they did. Or who knows WHERE I'd have let Michael's hands go next).

Actually, this was even MORE EMBARRASSING than THAT time, believe it or not. Because, I mean – dancing! With another guy!

Which I don't even know if they saw, because they were like, 'Sorry, don't mind us,' and hurried down the hall to their room before any of us could practically even say hello.

Still. Every time I think of what they MIGHT have seen, I go all hot and cold – the way Alec Guinness said he always felt every time he saw himself in the scene in *Star Wars: A New Hope* where Obi-Wan talks about feeling a great disturbance in the Force, as if millions of voices cried out in terror and were suddenly silenced.

Worse, as soon as the Drs Moscovitz were gone – I totally stopped dancing when I saw them; in fact, I froze – Lilly came up to me and whispered, 'Were you supposed to be sexy dancing or something? Because you sort of looked like someone stuck an ice cube down your shirt and you were trying to shake it out.'

Sexy dancing! Lilly thought I was sexy dancing! With J.P.! In front of Michael!

After that, of course, it was impossible to keep up my party-girl charade. I fully went and sat down by myself on the couch.

And Michael didn't even come over to ask me if I'd lost my mind or challenge J.P. to a duel or anything. Instead, he followed his parents, I guess to see if they'd come back early because something was wrong, or if the conference had just ended early, or what.

I sat there for like two minutes, listening to everyone around me laughing and having a good time, and feeling my palms break into a cold sweat. I was surrounded by people – surrounded by them! – but I swear I had never felt more alone in my life. Sexy dancing! I'd been sexy dancing! With another boy!

Even Lilly had stopped filming me, finding the sight of Doo Pak tasting Cool Ranch Doritos for the first time much more interesting than my intense mortification.

J.P. was the only one who said a word to me after that – besides Tina, on the couch opposite mine, who leaned over and said, 'That was a very nice dance, Mia,' like I'd been doing some kind of performance piece, or something.

'Hey,' J.P. said, coming over to where I was sitting. 'I think you forgot this.'

I looked at what he was holding. My three-quarters-empty beer! The substance responsible for my having thought it might be a good idea to do a sexy dance with another boy in the first place!

'Take it away!' I moaned, and buried my face in my knees.

'Oh,' J.P. said. 'Sorry. Um . . . are you all right?'

'No,' I said, to my thighs.

'Is there anything I can do?' he asked.

'Can you create a rift in the space–time continuum so no one will remember what an ass I just made of myself?'

'Um. I don't think so. How did you make an ass of yourself?'

Which was sweet of him – to pretend he hadn't noticed, and all. But seriously, that just made it worse.

Which is why I did the only thing I thought I reasonably could: I gathered up my things – and my bodyguard – and left before anybody could see me cry.

Which I did all the way home.

And now all I can do is hope that J.P. was lying and

that he really does know how to create a rift in the space–time continuum that will make it so that everyone who was at that party forgets I was ever there too.

Especially Michael.

Who by now has to be way more than slightly aware that I am, in the worst sense of the word, a party girl.

Oh, God.

I think I need an aspirin.

Sunday, March 7, 9 a.m., the Loft

No messages from Michael. No email. No calls.

It's official: he is disgusted even to know me.

And I don't blame him one bit. I'd go throw myself into the East River in shame if I didn't have a rehearsal.

I just called Zabar's and, using my mom's credit card (um, unbeknown to her, since she's still sleeping, and Mr G has taken Rocky out to buy orange juice), ordered bagels and lox to be delivered to the Moscovitzes' apartment, as my way of saying I'm sorry.

No one can stay mad after an everything bagel from Zabar's.

Right?

Sexy dancing! What was I THINKING?????

Sunday, March 7, 5 p.m., Ballroom at the Plaza

We never should have worried about memorizing our lines by Monday. I know them cold already, we've been through this play so many times.

And my feet are killing me from all the (not sexy) dancing. Feather says we all have to get something called jazz shoes. She's bringing a bunch for us tomorrow.

Except that by tomorrow, my feet will have fallen off.

Also, my throat is starting to hurt from all the singing. Madame Puissant has us sipping hot cups of Emer'gen-C.

Phil, the pianist, looks ready to drop. Even Grandmere is starting to droop. Only Señor Eduardo, dozing in his chair, looks rested. Well, Señor Eduardo and Rommel.

Oh, God. She's making them run through, 'Genovia, My Genovia' one more time. I freaking HATE this song. At least I'm not in this number. Still. Can't she see she's driving us past breaking point? My God, aren't there rules about how long you can force a child to work?

Oh, well. At least all this is keeping my mind off last night's humiliation. Sort of. I mean, Lilly still brings it up every chance she gets – 'Oh, Mia, hey, thanks for the bagels,' and, 'Hey, Mia, maybe you could work that sexy dance into the scene where you murder Alboin,' and, 'Where's your beret?'

Which of course has everyone who wasn't there going, 'What's she talking about?' To which Lilly just smiles all knowingly.

And then there's the Michael thing. Lilly says he wasn't even there to GET the bagels I sent over this morning. He went back to his dorm room last night after the party ended, because his parents were home and didn't need him to keep Lilly out of trouble any more.

I've sent him like three text messages apologizing for being such a spaz.

All I got back from him was this:

WE NEED 2 TALK

Which can only mean one thing, of course. He—

Oh, wait. J.P. just passed me a note, so we won't get yelled at for whispering, as happened earlier when he leaned over to let me know my combat boot had come untied.

Hey. You aren't mad at me, are you?

Me: Why would I be mad at you?

J.P.: For dancing with you.

Me: Why would I be mad at you for DANCING with me?

J.P.: Well, if it got you in trouble with your boyfriend or anything.

It was looking more and more like it totally had. But that wasn't anybody's fault but mine . . . certainly not J.P.'s.

Me: No. That was totally NICE of you. It helped me

not to look like the biggest freak in the universe.
I'm so STUPID. I can't believe I had that beer.
I was just so nervous, you know. Of not being
enough of a party girl.

J.P.: Well, you looked like you were having a great time,
if it's any consolation. Not like today. Today you
look – well, that's why I thought you might be mad
at me. Either because of last night, or maybe
because of that thing I said the other day, about
knowing you're a vegetarian because of that fit you
had in the caff that one time.

Me: No. Why would that make me mad? It's true.
I DID have a fit when I found out they put meat in
the lasagne. I mean, it was *supposed* to be
vegetarian.

J.P.: I know. They screw EVERYTHING up in that
cafeteria. Have you seen what they do to the chilli?

Me: You mean how they put corn in it sometimes?

J.P.: Yeah, exactly. That is just wrong. There shouldn't
be corn in chilli. It's unnatural. Don't you think?

Me: Well, I never really thought about it before.
I mean, I like corn.

J.P.: Well, I don't. I never have. Not since – whatever.
Never mind.

Me: Not since what?

J.P.: No, it's nothing. Really. Never mind.

But of course, now I HAD to know.

Me: No, really. It's OK. You can tell me. I won't say a word to anyone. I swear.

J.P.: Well, it's just . . . you know how I told you the only celebrity I'd really like to meet is David Mamet?

Me: Yeah . . .

J.P.: Well, my parents have actually met him. They went to his house for a dinner party once about four years ago. And I was so excited when I found out, I was like – in that way you do, when you're twelve, you know, and you think the world revolves around you – 'Did you tell him about me, Dad? Did you tell him I'm his biggest fan?'

Me: Yeah. And what did your dad say?

J.P.: He said, 'Yes, son, as a matter of fact, your name did come up.' Turns out Dad had told him about me all right. He told him about the first time they ever fed me corn as a baby.

Me: Yeah?

J.P.: And how amazed they were the next morning when they found it in whole pieces in my diaper. The corn, I mean.

!!!!!!!!!!!!!!!!!!

Actually, this happened the first – and only – time we fed corn to Rocky. So I know PRECISELY how gross it really is.

Me: EWWWWWWWWWWWWWWWWWW! Oops, I mean. Sorry. That must have been very embarrassing. I mean, for you. That they told your idol something like that about you. Even if you WERE just a baby at the time that it happened.

J.P.: Embarrassing? I was mortified! I haven't been able to stand the sight of corn since!

Me: Well. That explains it then.

J.P.: Explains what?

Me: Nothing. Your aversion to corn, I mean.

J.P.: Yeah. Parents. They mess you up, you know?

Me: Tell me about it.

J.P.: Can't live with them. Can't afford to live without them. Speaking of which, what do you think of this poem:

They pay for your food
And lodging and school.
All they ask in return
Is that you follow their rules.

You have no control,
Your destiny's not your own,
At least till you're eighteen
And you can finally leave home.

Me: Whoa. That is good! You should submit it to Lilly's magazine!

J.P.: Thanks. I might submit it – along with the Principal Gupta poem. Are you going to have anything in it? Lilly's 'zine, I mean?

Me: No.

Because of course the only thing I've written lately (besides journal entries) is 'No More Corn!'. And I've already told Lilly she can't publish that. Something I'm especially glad of now, because I really don't think, considering that story J.P. just told me, about WHY he hates corn, that he would think it's funny. My short story about him, I mean.

Oh, God. Grandmere wants me for the strangulation scene.

I wish someone would strangle ME. Because then Michael and I wouldn't *need 2 talk*. Because I'd just be dead.

Sunday, March 7, 9 p.m., the Loft

I can't believe this. Why does everything have to go from bad to worse? First of all, I still haven't been able to reach Michael. He's not answering on his cell and he's not online, and Doo Pak says he's not in their room and that he has no idea where 'Mike' might be.

Except that I have a pretty good idea: as far away from me as he can possibly get.

Just my luck, too, that out of the two Moscovitz siblings, the one I *least* want to hear from is the one who won't stop IMing me. I just got this from Lilly in response to my reminder that I don't want her putting 'No More Corn!' in her magazine.

WomynRule: Um, sorry, it's staying in. It's my best piece. By the way, are you wearing your beret to the party?

>

FtLouie: Would you shut up about that stupid beret? And what party? What are you talking about? And, Lilly, you can't publish my story without my permission. And I'm retracting my permission for you to publish it.

>

WomynRule: THE AIDE DE FERME PARTY YOUR GRANDMOTHER IS HAVING. And you can't. Because once a piece is submitted to the editorial offices of *Fat Louie's Pink Butthole*, it becomes the property of *Fat Louie's Pink Butthole*.

```
>
```

FtLouie: OK, a) stop calling it that, and b)
            THERE ARE NO EDITORIAL OFFICES FOR
            YOUR MAGAZINE. THE EDITORIAL
            OFFICES ARE YOUR BEDROOM. And Aide
            de Ferme is a benefit, not a party.

```
>
```

WomynRule: I meant offices in the figurative
            sense. Now, seriously. If you
            aren't wearing your beret, can I?

This is horrible. Poor J.P.!

What is UP with the Moscovitz siblings? I mean, I can understand Michael hating me, but why is Lilly being such a freak about this story thing?

If I weren't so exhausted I'd order the limo to come back and take me over to Lilly's first, so I could beat some sense into her, and then up to Michael's, so I could apologize in person.

But I'm too tired to do anything but take a bath and go to bed.

I seriously don't know how Paris Hilton does it – TV appearances, managing her own jewellery and make-up line, AND partying every night to all hours? No wonder she lost her dog that one time and thought it had been kidnapped . . .

Though the chances of me ever losing Fat Louie are slim to none, since he's way too heavy to carry around on a little pillow the way Paris carries Tinkerbell. Besides which, if I even tried something like that, he'd claw my face off.

Monday, March 8, Homeroom

So this morning I 'borrowed' my mom's credit card again and had one of those giant cookies sent to Michael. Only this time I made sure to send it to his dorm address. I am having the cookie makers write the word 'Sorry' in frosting on a twelve-inch chocolate-chocolate chip.

I realize sending a cookie – even a twelve-inch one with the word *Sorry* written on it in frosting – is a woefully inadequate way of expressing one's remorse for sexy dancing with another guy in front of one's boyfriend.

But I can't afford to get Michael what he really wants, which is a ride on the space shuttle.

After I ordered the cookie, I walked out of my room and found Rocky hanging on to fistfuls of Fat Louie's fur and shrieking, 'Kee! Kee! Kee!'

Poor Fat Louie looked as if he had just swallowed a sock.

But really what he had swallowed was his impulse to slash my baby brother to ribbons. Fat Louie is such a good cat, he was just LETTING Rocky hang on to him.

But that didn't mean he didn't have a look of naked panic on his big orange face. I could tell that in ten more seconds he'd have cracked like an eggshell.

I came to the rescue of course and was like, *'Mom! Can't you watch your child for ONE SINGLE SOLITARY MINUTE?'*

But Mom hadn't even had her coffee yet and so was incapable of controlling her kid, much less actually seeing anything that wasn't happening unless it involved Barbara Bellerieve on the TV screen in front of her.

She has no idea how lucky she is that I came along when I did. If Fat Louie HAD lost control of himself and let loose on Rocky, he could have sustained cat scratch disease and died. Rocky could have, I mean. Cat scratch disease is a super-serious and totally under-reported illness. It can cause anorexia, if you aren't careful.

Not, in Rocky's case, that anyone would notice, since he is roughly the size of your average four-year-old, even though he's not even a year old yet.

In fact, if Rocky, like Fat Louie, were orange, he'd look exactly like an Oompa-Loompa.

I seriously don't see how, between my baby brother, my friends, my parents, this princess thing, my grandmother and this sexy dancing business, I am ever going to achieve self-actualization.

Monday, March 8, PE

Lana came up to me as I was in the shower just now and asked me where her tickets for the Aide de Ferme benefit were. I was so tired – and my forearms are so sore from strangling Boris, let alone smacking that stupid volleyball, even though I only did it once . . . the rest of the time, I just ducked when I saw it coming at me – I went, 'Don't get your panties in a wad, I submitted everyone's name to my grandmother's party organizer, OK? You and Trish will get in. You just have to show up.'

She looked kind of startled. I guess I WAS kind of sharp.

You know, it's becoming clearer and clearer to me that actresses get a really bum rap. You know, the ones with the rumoured 'temperaments'. I mean, like Cameron Diaz and stuff. If she has HALF as much stress as I do, it's no wonder she freaks out and kicks photographers and breaks their cameras and all.

It just goes to show that what one person considers a 'bad attitude' might actually just be total frustration over being pushed beyond the brink of one's mental and physical endurance.

That's all I'm saying.

Monday, March 8, US Economics

Elasticity

Elasticity is the degree to which a demand or supply curve reacts to a change in price.

Elasticity varies among products based on how essential that product is to the consumer.

I am thinking I lost a lot of elasticity in Michael's eyes after that whole sexy dancing thing.

Or maybe it was the beret.

Monday, March 8, English

Everyone is too tired to talk or even pass notes.

Also, apparently none of us read *O Pioneers!* over the weekend.

Ms Martinez says she is really disappointed in us.

Get in line, Ms M. Get in line.

Monday, March 8, Lunch

J.P. is sitting with us again. He is the only one at the table (who is in the play – I mean, musical – anyway) who isn't catatonic with exhaustion. He's even written a new poem. It goes:

> I always wanted
> To be in a play,
> But the thrill of running lines
> Grows fainter by the day
>
> Now that I'm here,
> I just want a reversal,
> I'm sick of blocking,
> Sick of rehearsal
>
> Someone please help us,
> Hear our pleas as they're made
> Get us out of this mess –
> I mean, musical – *Braid!*

Funny. I'd laugh, if my diaphragm didn't hurt so much from lifting up that stupid piano.

Still no word from Michael. I know he's got his History of Dystopic Sci-Fi in Film midterm right now. So that would explain why he hasn't called to thank me for the cookie.

It isn't because he never wants to hear from or see me again, on account of the sexy dance.

Probably.

Monday, March 8, G and T

OK, she's gone mental.

Seriously. What's WRONG with her? She expects us all to help her put her stupid literary magazine together – literally: she just wheeled in 3,700 pages that we are apparently supposed to collate and staple – but she still won't pull 'No More Corn!'

'Lilly,' I said. 'PLEASE. We know J.P. now. We're FRIENDS with him. You can't run the story. It's just going to hurt his feelings. I mean, I have him KILL himself at the end.'

'J.P. is a poet,' is all Lilly said back.

'SO? WHAT DOES THAT HAVE TO DO WITH ANYTHING?'

'Poets kill themselves all the time. It's a statistical fact. Amongst writers, poets have the shortest life expectancy. They are more likely to kill themselves than writers of prose or non-fiction. J.P. will probably agree with the way you've ended "No More Corn!" since that's the way he's going to go someday anyway.'

'Lilly!'

But she won't be swayed.

I have refused to help collate and staple on ethical grounds, so she's got Boris doing it.

You can tell he doesn't want to. He's just too tired to practise his violin.

You know, I'm starting to wonder if selling candles wouldn't have been simpler than all this.

Monday, March 8, Earth Science

Kenny wasn't too tired last night to do our lab worksheet.

But he WAS too tired not to spill marinara sauce all
over it.

I recopied it for free. I've officially given up on Alfred
Marshall. He may work for Grandmere and Lana, but
he hasn't done squat for me.

Still no word from Michael. And his History of Dystopic
Sci-Fi in Film midterm should be over by now.

I think it's official.

He hates me.

Homework:

Homeroom: N/A
PE: WASH GYM SHORTS!!! I CAN'T BELIEVE I
FORGOT
US Economics: who knows? Too tired to care
English: D/C (don't care)
French: D/C
G and T: as if
Geometry: D/C
Earth Science: D/C (Kenny will tell me)

Monday, March 8, Limo on the way home from the Plaza

I can't believe it.

Really. It's too much. After all that . . .

OK. I have to get a grip. MUST. GET. A. GRIP.

It started out innocently enough. We were all lying there on the ballroom floor, exhausted from our final run-through.

Then somebody – I think it was Tina – went, 'Um, Your Highness? My parents want to know where they can buy tickets to this show, so they can be sure to see it.'

'All your parents' names have already been put on the guest-list,' Grandmere said, from where she sat, enjoying a post-rehearsal cigarette (apparently, she's allowing herself to smoke after run-throughs, as well as after meals), 'for Wednesday.'

'Wednesday?' Tina asked, a funny inflection in her voice.

'That is correct,' Grandmere said, exhaling a plume of blue smoke. Señor Eduardo coughed a little in his sleep as some of it drifted his way.

'But isn't this Wednesday the night of the Aide de Ferme benefit?' someone else – I think it was Boris – asked.

'That is correct,' Grandmere said, again.

And that's when it finally sunk in.

Lilly was the first one up.

'WHAT?' she cried. 'You're going to make us do this play in front of all the people coming to your PARTY?'

208

'It's a musical,' Grandmere replied darkly. 'Not a play.'

'You said, when I asked you last week, that we'd be putting *Braid!* on a week from that day!' Lilly shouted. 'And that was Thursday!'

Grandmere puffed on her cigarette. 'Oh dear,' she said, not sounding in the least concerned. 'I was off by one day, wasn't I?'

'I am *not*,' Boris said, drawing himself up to his full height, 'going to be strangled by some girl's hair in front of Joshua Bell.'

'And *I* am not,' Lilly declared, 'going to play someone's mistress in front of Madonna – no matter how charitable she is !'

'I don't want to play a maid in front of celebrities,' Tina said meekly.

Grandmere very calmly stubbed her cigarette out on an empty plate someone had left on top of the piano. I saw Phil eyeing the smoking butt nervously from where he sat at the keyboard. Obviously he is as nervous about contracting lung cancer from second-hand smoke as I am.

'So this,' Grandmere said, her Gitanes-roughened voice projecting very loudly across the empty ballroom, 'is the thanks I get, for taking your dull, average little lives and injecting them with glamour and art.'

'Um,' Boris said. 'My life already has art in it. I don't know if you're aware of this, Your Majesty, but I'm a concert violinist, and I—'

'I tried,' Grandmere's voice rang out as she ignored him, 'to do something to enrich your humdrum days of scholastic slavery. I tried to give you something meaningful, something you could look forward to. And this is how you repay me. By whining that you don't want to share what we've worked so hard to create together with others. What kind of ACTORS are you?????'

Everyone blinked at her. Because, of course, none of us considered him- or herself an actor of any kind.

'Were you not,' Grandmere demanded, 'put on this earth with a God-given obligation to share your talent with others? Would you dare to presume to DEFY God's plan for you by DENYING the world the right to see you perform your art? Is THAT what you're trying to tell me? That you want to DEFY God?'

Only Lilly was brave enough to answer.

'Um,' she said. 'Your Highness, I don't believe I am defying God – if She does, in fact, exist – by saying that I don't care to make an ass out of myself in front of a bunch of world leaders and movie stars.'

'Too late!' Grandmere cried. 'You've already done it! Because only an ASS gets embarrASSed. Where do you think the word comes from, anyway? A true artist is never embarrassed by her work. NEVER.'

'Fine,' Lilly said. 'I'm not embarrassed. But—'

'This show,' Grandmere went on, 'into which all of you have poured your life's blood, is too important not to be shared with as many people as we possibly can. And what venue could possibly be as fitting for its one and only performance than a benefit that is being held to raise money for the poor olive growers of Genovia? Don't you see, people? *Braid!* bears a message – a message of hope – that it is vital people – especially Genovia's farmers – hear. In these dark times, our show illustrates that evil-doers will ultimately never win, and that even the weakest among us can play a role in thwarting them.

Were we to deny people this message, would we not, in essence, be letting the evil-doers win?'

'Oh, brother,' I heard Lilly mutter under her breath.

But everybody else looked pretty inspired. Everybody but me, that is. Because, while I'm all for helping out the Genovian olive growers, how is any of this going to help me and my fiscal crisis? I had to trust that Grandmere hadn't forgotten our agreement.

Wait . . . trust? Grandmere? I was so dead.

It wasn't until it sunk in with everyone else that Wednesday night is the day after tomorrow that they, like me, began to freak.

And some of us – OK, Kenny – still don't even know the choreography.

Which is why Grandmere said to be prepared for tomorrow night's rehearsal to go on all night long, if necessary.

Still, Grandmere's speech WAS pretty inspiring. We really CAN'T let the evil-doers win.

Even if the evil-doers happen to be . . . well, ourselves.

Which is why I've just told Hans to take me to Engle Hall, the dorm where Michael lives at Columbia. I am going to get him to forgive me if I have to grovel on the floor like Rommel when he realizes it's bathtime.

Monday, March 8, the Limo home from Michael's dorm

Wow. Wow, wow, wow, wow, wow, wow, wow, wow, wow, wow, wow.

That is all I can think of to say.

Also: I'm such an idiot.

Seriously. I mean, all the clues were there, and I just didn't put them together.

OK, maybe if I write it all down in a lucid manner, I'll be able to process it.

So I walked into Engle Hall, where Michael lives, and buzzed his room from the lobby. He was actually home for a change – thank God. He seemed kind of surprised when he heard my voice on the intercom, but he said he'd be right down, because campus security officers guard the doors to the hall and won't let anybody past the lobby and into the building unless they're escorted by a resident. Not even princesses and their bodyguard. The resident has to come down and sign them in, and the guests have to leave ID and stuff.

I took the fact that Michael was willing even to come down and sign me in as a good sign.

Until I saw him.

Then I realized there was nothing good about it at all.

Because Michael looked REALLY sad about something. I mean, REALLY sad.

And I started getting a very bad feeling.

Because I know he has midterms this week and all. Which would be enough to depress anyone.

But Michael didn't look midterm-depressed.

He looked more I-just-found-out-my-girlfriend-is-astark-raving-lunatic-and-I-have-to-break-up-with-her-now depressed.

But I thought maybe I was just, you know. Projecting, or whatever.

Still, the whole way up to his room in the elevator, I was rehearsing in my mind what to say. You know, how I should act when he brought up the Sexy Dance. And the beer. I was thinking it shouldn't be too hard for me to convince him that I had been suffering from a temporary hormonal imbalance at the time, on account of how I should be used to acting by now, since I've been doing it all week.

Plus, you know, I'm the world's biggest liar.

But the J.P. thing. That was going to be harder to explain. Because I wasn't sure I even understood it myself.

Then, when we got to Michael's floor, Lars discreetly took a seat in the TV lounge, where there was a game on, and Michael and I went to his room, which was fortunately empty, his room-mate, Doo Pak, being at a meeting of the Korean Student Association.

'So,' I said, trying to sound all casual after sitting down on Michael's neatly made bed. Even though the last thing I felt was casual. In fact, I felt as if all the blood in my veins had frozen up. If someone had chopped my arm off at that moment, I'm pretty sure it would have shattered into a thousand pieces instead of bled, like I was one of those frozen guys in that cryogenic prison in *Demolition Man* (also a dystopic sci-fi film).

Because, suddenly, I was sure Michael was going to break up with me for being such an immature freak at his party.

And the next thing I knew, I heard myself blurting,

'Look, I'm sorry about the stupid sexy dance. Really, really sorry. And there's nothing going on between me and J.P.. Seriously. It's just that I was FREAKING OUT. I mean, all those super-smart college girls—'

Michael, who'd taken a seat across from me in his desk chair, blinked. 'Sexy dance?'

'Yes,' I said. 'The one I was doing with J.P.'

Michael raised his eyebrows. 'Was *that* what you were doing? A sexy dance?'

'Yes.' I could feel my cheeks heating up. Can I just say that when Buffy did a sexy dance at the Bronze to make Angel jealous in that one episode of *Buffy the Vampire Slayer*, I'm pretty sure Angel went out and killed a bunch of vampires afterwards just to work out his sexual frustration? Trust MY boyfriend to not even recognize a sexy dance when he saw one.

I tried not to think about what this suggested for the future of our relationship. Not to mention my sexy-dancing skills.

'It's not totally my fault,' I insisted. 'Well, I mean, the sexy dance part was. But you invite me to this party knowing I'll be the youngest, least intelligent person there. How did you EXPECT me to feel? I was totally intimidated!'

'Mia,' Michael said a little dryly. 'You were by far not the least intelligent person there. And you're a princess. And *you* were intimidated?'

'Well,' I said. 'I may be a princess, but I still get intimidated. Especially by older girls. College girls. Who know about . . . college things. And I'm sorry I spazzed. But was what I did really so unforgivable? I mean, all I did was have ONE beer and do a sexy dance with another guy. And I wasn't even technically dancing with him, just sort of in front of him. And OK, maybe ultimately it wasn't that sexy. And I do realize now that the beret was a mistake. The whole thing was totally immature, I know. But—' I could feel tears welling in my eyes. 'But you still could have called instead of giving me the silent treatment for two days!'

'The silent treatment?' Michael echoed. 'What are you talking about? I haven't been giving you the silent treatment, Mia.'

'Excuse me,' I said, fighting to keep from bursting into tears. 'I left you like fifty messages, plus sent you bagels AND a giant cookie, and all I heard from you is this cryptic text, *We need 2 talk*—'

'Give me a break, Mia,' Michael said. Now he looked kind of annoyed. 'I've been slightly preoccupied—'

'I realize your History of Dystopic Sci-Fi in Film course is very intense and all,' I interrupted. 'And I know I acted like a fool at your party. But the least you could have done was—'

'I haven't been preoccupied with homework, Mia,' Michael said, interrupting me right back. 'And yes, you *did* act like a fool at my party. But that's not it, either. The fact is, I've been trying to deal with total family drama. My parents . . . they're separating.'

Um. **WHAT?????**

I blinked at him. I didn't think I could have heard him right. 'Excuse me?' I said.

'Yeah.' Michael stood up and, turning his back to me, ran a hand through his thick dark hair. 'My parents are calling it quits. They told me the night of the party.' He turned to face me, and I saw that, even though he was trying not to let it show, he was upset. Really upset.

And not because his girlfriend isn't a party girl. Or because she's TOO much of one. Not because of either of those things at all.

'I'd have told you then,' he said. 'If you'd stuck around. But I came out of their room and you were gone.'

I stared at him in horror, realizing the true magnitude of my stupidity that night. I had fled his party, embarrassed about having got caught doing a sexy dance with another guy by Michael's parents, and assuming he'd felt the same way about it . . . Why else had he gone off and left me alone like that?

But now I realized he'd had a good reason to disappear the way he had. He'd been talking to his parents. Who hadn't been telling him to break up with his slutty, sexy-dancing girlfriend.

Instead, they'd been telling him *they* were splitting up.

'It wasn't a conference they went to this past weekend,' Michael went on. 'They lied to me. They went to a marathon session with a marriage counsellor. It was a last-ditch effort to see if they could iron things out. Which failed.'

I stared at him. I felt like someone had kicked me in the chest. I couldn't quite catch my breath.

'Ruth and Morty?' I heard myself whisper. 'Separating?'

'Ruth and Morty,' he confirmed. 'Separating.'

I thought back to something Lilly had said that day we bumped our heads in the limo. *I think Ruth and Morty have bigger things to worry about,* she'd said.

I flung a startled look at Michael. 'Does Lilly know?'

'My parents are waiting for the right time to tell her,'

Michael said. 'They didn't even want to tell *me*, except that – well, I could tell something was wrong. Anyway, they seem to think with this magazine Lilly's working on, and this play you guys are in –'

'Musical,' I said.

'– that she seems stressed right now, so they thought they'd tell her later. I don't necessarily agree with their decision, but they asked me to let them do it their own way. So please don't say anything to her.'

'I think she knows,' I said. 'In the limo the other day . . . she said something.'

'I wouldn't be surprised,' Michael said. 'She has to have at least suspected. I mean, she's been home with the two of them fighting all year, while I've been here at the dorm, sort of removed from it.'

'Oh, God,' I said, feeling a stab of pity for Lilly. Suddenly, I understood why she was being so weird about the literary magazine thing. I mean, if she knew her parents were splitting up, that would totally explain her mood swings and general weirdness.

Too bad I didn't have any such excuse for MY weirdness.

'Michael,' I said. 'I had no idea. I thought . . . I thought you were mad at me because I acted like such a head case the other night. I thought you were disgusted with me. Or disappointed in me. Because I'm not a party girl.'

'Mia,' Michael said, shaking his head – almost as if HE couldn't believe any of this was happening either. 'I *was* mad at you. I don't *want* a party girl. All I want is—'

But before he could say anything else, the door to his dorm room opened, and Doo Pak came in, looking cheerful as ever . . . especially when he saw me.

'Oh, hello, Princess!' he cried. 'I was thinking you are here, since I see Mr Lars in the lounge! How are you doing tonight? Thank you for the giant *Sorry* cookie. It was very delicious. Mike and I have been eating it all day.'

I was going to say, 'You're welcome.' I was going to say, 'I'm great, Doo Pak. How are you?'

Which wasn't what I WANTED to say. What I WANTED to say was, 'Get out, Doo Pak! Get out! Michael, finish what you were saying. All you want is *what*? ALL YOU WANT IS WHAT???'

Because, you know, it had sounded like it might be slightly important – especially considering the, 'I *was* mad at you,' part right before it.

But then the phone rang, and Doo Pak picked it up and said, 'Oh, hello, Mrs Moscovitz! Yes, Mike is here. You wish to speak to him? Here, Mike.'

And even though Michael was making slashing motions under his chin and mouthing, 'I'm not here,' at Doo Pak, it was too late. He had to take the phone and go, 'Um, Mom? Yeah, hi. Now's not a real good time, could I call you back later?'

But I heard his mother droning on and on.

And Michael, always the dutiful son, listened.

While I sat there thinking: Dr and Dr Moscovitz, splitting up? It CAN'T be. It's not possible. It's just not NATURAL for them to split. It's like . . . well, it's like Michael and I splitting up.

Which we might actually be doing. Because, you know, he never actually did say he forgave me. For the J.P. thing. He admitted he *was* mad at me, but never said if he was STILL mad.

Oh my God. Are the Moscovitzes not the only couple breaking up right now?

Except there was no way I could actually find out. At least, not just then, since Michael was holding the phone to his face, going, 'Mom. Mom, I know. Don't worry.'

And I knew then that what was going on with him – and with us – was more than a *Sorry* cookie could solve.

I also knew there was nothing else I could do.

Which was why I got up and left.

Because what else was I supposed to do?

From the desk of
Her Royal Highness Princess Amelia Mignonette
Grimaldi Thermopolis Renaldo

Dear Dr Carl Jung,

I realize that you are still dead. However, things have suddenly got much worse.

And now I'm not worried so much about transcending my ego and achieving self-actualization.

Instead, I'm worried about my friends.

Not that I don't have my own problems, of course. But now I've learned that my boyfriend's parents are splitting up. Dr Jung, this could devastate a young man in his prime like Michael. Not only is it clearly breaking his heart, but it could give him abandonment issues that I fear will have a trickle-down effect into MY relationship with him. I mean, what if, from his parents' example, Michael learns that walking away from a relationship is the way to handle conflict?

This could totally happen. I know because I saw it once on *Dr Phil*.

And the fact is, there is conflict going on in our relationship RIGHT now, due to an ill-timed sexy dance on my part.

Could things possibly GET any worse?
PLEASE SEND HELP.

Your friend,
Mia Thermopolis

Tuesday, March 9, Midnight, the Loft

You know what this reminds me of? 'No More Corn!'
Seriously. The part where the nameless main character
is wandering the streets of Manhattan, surrounded by
people and yet, ultimately, so very, very alone. So alone
that he realizes he has no choice but to step in front of
that F train.

Which if you think about it is a very selfish thing to
do since the poor conductor driving the train will be
traumatized for life because of it.

Still. It is like my life has started imitating my ART!!!
Seriously!!! My fictional story is coming true – only not
for J.P.

For ME.

The thing is, as soon as I got in the limo, I sent
Michael a long email via Lars's Sidekick, telling him
how much I loved him, and how sorry I was, both about
his parents and for my being so immature and self-
centered. And for the sexy dance.

I fully expected to get an long email back from him
by the time I got home, saying he loved me too and that
he forgave me for being such a weirdo at his party.

But he didn't write back.

At all.

I can't believe this. I mean, what do I do NOW? I
already sent him a *Sorry* cookie. I have no idea what to
do next. I'd buy him a ride on the space shuttle if I
thought it would help. But I don't think it would.

Besides, I can't afford a ride on the space shuttle. I
can't even afford a TOY space shuttle.

As if all that weren't enough, Michael's parting words

to me keep echoing in my head: 'Mia, I don't want a party girl. All I want is—'

All I want is . . . WHAT?

I will probably never know. But I can't help worrying that, whatever it is Michael wants, I'm not it.

And right now, I can't say I blame him.

Tuesday, March 9, the Limo on the way to school

So Lilly was all, 'Oh, my God, what happened to YOU?' when she got into the car.

And I was like, 'What do you mean?'

And she was like, 'You look like crap. What, did you not get any sleep last night or something? Your grand-mother is going to kill you, we have the dress rehearsal tonight.'

So obviously she doesn't know that I know about her parents. It's possible that Michael was wrong, and Lilly really doesn't know about them.

Unless she's actually as fine an actress as she thinks she is.

Which means I can't tell her why I look like crap. I mean, Lilly would only SLIGHTLY kill me for knowing her parents are splitting up before SHE even knows her parents are splitting up. Besides, Michael asked me to keep it to myself.

I guess I could tell her that I think Michael and I are breaking up on account of my sexy dance with J.P.

But isn't that just a little more than she should have to deal with right now? I mean, if she DOES know about her parents? Is it really fair for me to expect her to cope with their break-up AS WELL AS mine? If that's even what's going on with Michael and me?

No. No, it is not.

So instead of telling her the truth, I just went, 'I don't know. I think I'm getting a cold.'

'Bummer,' Lilly said. And then she told me how she'd got almost twenty of her 'zines completely collated and stapled. Only nine hundred and eighty to go. Because of course Lilly thinks every single person in the entire school is going to buy one.

I didn't bother to contradict her. For one thing, I feel totally empty inside, so it's not like I even care.

And for another, she was totally mean to me when I asked her, AGAIN, to pull 'No More Corn!'. She was like, 'Where would we be today if Woodward and Bernstein had asked the *Post* to pull their story on Watergate? Huh? Where would we be?'

But breaking the Watergate scandal is COMPLETELY different to 'No More Corn!'. One thing was going to bring down a presidency. The other is going to hurt someone's feelings. Which is more important?

Whatever. Lilly was just like, 'Your piece is the COVER STORY. It's right there, under *Fat Louie's Pink Butthole: A short story by AEHS's own princess, Mia Thermopolis.* I can't PULL it, not without having to redo the COVER, not to mention the table of contents. I'd have to redesign the cover, then print it, then photocopy a thousand pages ALL OVER AGAIN. I'm NOT doing it. I'm just NOT.'

I told her I'd help her with the photocopying. But she just shook her head.

I can't believe she's willing to hurt a friend just because she's too lazy to stand at the Xerox machine a little longer. And after all the things I've done for her too. Like protecting her fragile mental state from the truth about her parents, and possibly from the truth about Michael and me.

Sheesh.

Tuesday, March 9, Homeroom

I still can't believe it. I mean, it's like Wilma and Fred
Flintstone splitting. Or Homer and Marge Simpson. Or
Lana Weinberger and Josh Richter.

Well, except I wasn't bummed when THEY split up.

COUPLES YOU WOULD BE TOTALLY BUMMED TO FIND OUT WERE BREAKING UP:

Sarah Michelle Gellar and Freddie Prinze Jr.
Kelly Ripa and Mark Consuelos
Jessica Simpson and Nick Lachey
Scooby-Doo and Shaggy
Melissa Etheridge and Tammy Lynn Michaels
Bruce Springsteen and Patti Scialfa
Russell and Kimora Lee Simmons
Ben Affleck and Matt Damon
Danny DeVito and Rhea Perlman
Will and Jada Pinkett Smith
Queen Elizabeth and Prince Philip
Tom Hanks and Rita Wilson
Kevin Bacon and Kyra Sedgwick
Gwen Stefani and Gavin Rossdale
Ellen DeGeneres and Portia di Rossi
Hermione and Ron
Jay-Z and Beyoncé
Tea Leoni and David Duchovny
Sandy and Kirsten Cohen
Tina Hakim Baba and Boris Pelkowski
My mom and Mr G

I can't believe the Moscovitzes are breaking up. I mean, they're JUNGIAN PSYCHIATRISTS. If they can't make a relationship work, what hope do the rest of us have?

From the desk of
Her Royal Highness Princess Amelia Mignonette
Grimaldi Thermopolis Renaldo

Dear Dr Carl Jung,

Well, I get it now. I totally get it.

It took me a while. I'll admit it. But the truth has finally sunk in.

It's funny how all this time, I thought transcendence would make me happy. You know, that through finally knowing my true self I'd gain total happiness at last. Boy, did you have me fooled. You must be laughing your butt off up there in heaven or wherever you are. Because you knew all along, didn't you? You knew the truth.

And that's that there *is* no Jungian tree of self-actualization. There *is* no transcendence of the ego. The Drs Moscovitz splitting up just proves this.

The truth is, you're all alone.

And then you die.

Don't worry. I get it now.

This is the last letter I'll be writing to you. Goodbye forever.

Your former friend,
Mia Thermopolis

Tuesday, March 9, US Economics

Marginal utility = the additional satisfaction, or amount of utility, gained from each extra unit of consumption. Marginal utility decreases with each additional increase in the consumption of a good.

In other words, the less you have of something, the more you want it.

A phenomenon with which I am all too familiar.

Tuesday, March 9, English

Mia, are you OK? You look as if you might be coming down with something.

Oh, I'm great, Tina. Just great.

Oh.

OK, I'm lying. Michael is upset about my sexy dance with J.P. But he's MORE upset about something that has nothing whatsoever to do with me. Something I can't tell you. But he's barely speaking to me. I already sent him a *Sorry* cookie. I don't know what else to do.

Maybe you shouldn't do anything else. Boys aren't like girls, you know, Mia. They don't like to talk about their feelings. Probably the best thing you can do is just leave Michael alone. Whatever it is, he'll come around after he's worked through it. Like Boris and his Bartók.

Do you think so? It's so hard to just sit here and do nothing! And who doesn't want to TALK about their feelings????

I know. But that is just how boys are. They are like freaks of nature.

What are you two talking about?

230

Nothing.

Nothing.

Oh, right. Nothing, again. Whatever. Look. Lunch. Help me
collate?

Of course.

NO!!!! J.P. WILL SEE THE STORY ABOUT HIM!!!!
He sits with us at lunch now!

Yeah, what is up with that, anyway? Is this like a permanent
thing, or a just-until-the-show-is-over thing?

I think it's a Someone-Has-a-Crush-on-Mia Thing.

WHAT????

You think?

HE DOES NOT!!!!

I don't know, Mia. There is the sexy dance thing.
And I see him staring at you a lot when you're not
looking.

Um, how do you know it's not ME he's staring at, Tina?

Um . . . well, it COULD be you he's staring at, Lilly.
But I really thought—

Do you WANT him to be staring at you, Lilly?

I DIDN'T SAY THAT. I just asked how Tina can be so sure it's NOT me. I mean, you and I sit together a lot. It could be ME, not Mia, he has a crush on.

Oh my God. You like J.P.

I DO NOT!!!!!!

Yes, you do. You totally do.

OH MY GOD, COULD YOU BE MORE IMMATURE??? I AM NOT TAKING PART IN THIS CONVERSATION ANY MORE.

Oh my God. She totally likes him.

I know! Could she be more obvious about it?

It's so surprising. J.P. doesn't seem like her type.

Because he's good looking, English-speaking, and comes from a wealthy family?

Right. But he IS the creative type. And tall. And a very good dancer.

Wow. So I don't get it. If she likes him, why is she running that story of mine, that's only going to hurt his feelings?

I don't know. I love Lilly, but I can't really say I understand her.

Yeah. You could say that about ALL the Moscovitzes.

Oh, Mia. What are you going to do about Michael?

Do? Nothing. I mean, what CAN I do?

Wow. You're taking this current estrangement so well. I mean, apart from the fact that you look like you're about to throw up.

I AM throwing up, Tina. On the inside.

Tuesday, March 9, Lunch

Today at lunch J.P. was like, 'Are you all right, Mia?'

And I was like, 'Yeah. Why?'

And he was like, 'Because your colour's off.'

And I was like, 'My COLOUR? What are you talking about?'

And he was like, 'I don't know. You just don't look right.'

This does not sound like the kind of thing someone with a hidden burning passion for me would say.

So Tina must be wrong. It really must be Lilly J.P. likes after all.

That would be cool if they started going out. Because then it would give Lilly something to be happy about, you know, after she finds out the truth about her parents. And Michael and me.

Plus, maybe then Lilly would have less time to try to psychoanalyse me at the lunch table, like she's started doing right now.

Lilly: 'What's wrong, POG? Why haven't you
            finished your Devil Dog?'

Me: 'Because I'm not in the mood for a Devil
            Dog.'

Lilly: 'When have you ever not been in the mood
            for a Devil Dog?'

Me: 'Since today, OK?'

234

Rest of the table:	'Ooooooo.'

Me:	'I'm sorry. I didn't mean it like that.'

Lilly:	'See. We all know something's wrong, Thermopolis. Spill.'

Me:	'NOTHING IS WRONG. I'M JUST TIRED, OK?'

J.P:	'Hey, does anyone want to see my blisters? From my new jazz shoes? They're pretty sweet. Take a look.'

Is it my imagination, or was J.P. just trying to distract Lilly from picking on me?

God, he is SO nice.

I HAVE to get that story away from Lilly. Only how? HOW????

Tuesday, March 9, Gifted and Talented

Well. THAT didn't go well.

And OK, maybe I should have just dropped the whole thing about her liking him.

But still. She didn't have to tell Mrs Hill I was trying to sabotage her 'zine, then gather everything up and go staple by herself in the Teachers' Lounge.

I have the blood of many generations of strong, independent women coursing through my veins. How would one of them handle this situation? Besides strangling Lilly, I mean.

Tuesday, March 9, Third-floor stairwell

Kenny took the pass to the men's room, and a few minutes later I took the pass to the ladies', and we both ditched Earth Science and met Tina, who ditched Geometry, and Boris, who ditched English, and Ling Su, who ditched Art, up here to go over the choreography we haven't quite got yet.

I feel bad about ditching, and I recognize that getting an education is important.

But so is not making a fool of yourself in front of Bono.

Tuesday, March 9, Ballroom at the Plaza

When we walked into the Grand Ballroom this afternoon, there was a full orchestra tuning up there.

Also all these sound and lighting guys, running around, going, 'One, two, check. One, two, one, two, check.'

Also, there was a stage.

Yes. An actual stage had appeared at one end of the room.

It was like Ty and the cast of *Extreme Makeover: Home Edition* had come in the night and constructed this giant stage, complete with a full, rotating set containing castle walls, a beach scene, village shops and a blacksmith's forge.

It was incredible.

And so was Grandmere's bad mood when we walked in.

'You're late!' she screamed.

'Uh, yeah, sorry, Grandmere,' I said. 'There was a horse and carriage accident on Fifth Avenue.'

'What kind of professionals are you?' Grandmere, apparently choosing to ignore me, screamed. 'If this were a real Broadway show, you'd all be fired! There is no excuse for lateness on the stage!'

'Um,' J.P. said, 'the horse fell into a sinkhole. It took ten cab drivers to pull him out. He's going to be OK though.'

This information caused Grandmere to undergo a complete transformation. Or rather, the person who DELIVERED the information did.

'Oh, John Paul,' she said. 'I didn't see you standing

there. Come along, my dear, and meet the costume mistress. She's going to fit you into your smithy suit.'

!!!!!

Jeez!!! Never mind who J.P. likes, me or Lilly. It's pretty clear who GRANDMERE likes, anyway.

So we all got into our costumes and started the dress rehearsal. To keep our voices from being drowned out by all the violins and the horn section and stuff, we had to wear these little microphones, just like this was some kind of professional show or whatever. It felt really weird to be singing into a microphone – a REAL one, not just a hairbrush, which is what I usually sing into. Our voices really CARRY.

I'm sort of glad I practised lifting that piano with Madame Puissant so many times. Because at least now I can hit those high notes.

All that practising in the stairwell didn't help Kenny much, though, with the dancing. He's still hopeless. It's like his feet aren't attached to his legs or something, and don't obey commands from his brain. Grandmere is now making him stand back behind the chorus in the dance numbers.

Right now, she is giving us 'cast notes'. This is what she does after each run-through. She takes notes during the show, and instead of stopping it to correct something, she reads us each our notes at the end. Currently, she is instructing Lilly not to lift the train of her long dress with BOTH hands when she goes up the palace steps to greet Alboin. A lady, Grandmere says, would lift her train with ONE hand.

'But I'm not a lady,' Lilly is saying. 'I'm a prostitute, remember?'

'A mistress,' Grandmere says, 'is not a prostitute,

239

young lady. Was Camilla Parker Bowles a prostitute? Was Madame Chiang Kai-shek? Evita Peron? No. Some of the greatest female role models in the world started out as men's mistresses. That does not mean they ever prostituted themselves. And kindly do not argue with me. You will use only ONE HAND to lift your train.'

Now she's moving onto J.P.. Of course, everything HE does is perfect.

Although I really don't get how she thinks sucking up to John Paul Reynolds-Abernathy's kid is going to get him to back off on his bid for the faux island of Genovia.

But then, I've officially given up trying to second guess Grandmere. I mean, the woman is clearly an enigma wrapped in a mystery. Just when I think I've got her figured out, she comes up with some new whackadoo scheme.

So by now I should just be like, 'Why bother?' She's never going to tell me the true motivations behind most of her actions – like why she's so insistent that *I* play Rosagunde, and not someone who'd actually be good at it, like Lilly.

And she's never going to admit why she thinks this whole thing with being nice to J.P. is going to help her win her island. We just have to sit and listen to her while she goes, 'I really enjoyed that little bow you made during the final number, John Paul. But may I make a suggestion? I think it would be lovely if, after bowing, you swept Amelia into your arms and kissed her, with her body bent back – here, Feather, dear, show him what I mean –'

WAIT. WHAT????

Tuesday, March 9, Limo home from the Plaza

OH MY GOD!!!!!!!!!!! J.P. HAS TO KISS ME!!!!!!!!!!! IN THE PLAY!!!!!!!!!

I MEAN, MUSICAL!!!!!!!!!!!!!!

I can't believe this. I mean, the kiss isn't even in the script. Grandmere clearly just added it because – I don't even know why. It doesn't ADD anything to it. It's just this stupid kiss at the end between Rosagunde and Gustav.

I doubt it's even historically accurate.

But then, all the townspeople and the King of Italy gathering around after Rosagunde killed Alboin and singing about how happy they are that he's dead probably isn't historically accurate either.

Still. Grandmere KNOWS my heart belongs to another man – even if right now we might be sort of on the skids.

Still. What does she think she's doing, asking me to kiss someone else?

'For God's sake, Amelia,' she said, when I went up to her – QUIETLY, because of course I didn't want J.P. to know I wasn't one hundred per cent behind the whole kissing thing. I don't want to betray my boyfriend by kissing another guy (especially a guy he watched me sexy dance with not even a week ago) but I don't want to hurt J.P.'s feelings either – and asked if she had lost her mind.

'People expect a kiss between the male and female leads at the end of a musical,' Grandmere snapped. 'It's cruel to disappoint them.'

'But, Grandmere—'

'And please don't try to tell me that you feel kissing

241

John Paul is a huge betrayal of your love for That Boy.' *That Boy* is what Grandmere calls Michael. 'It's called ACTING, Amelia. Do you think Sir Laurence Olivier minded when his wife, Vivien Leigh, was called upon to kiss Clark Gable in *Gone with the Wind*? Certainly not. He understood it was ACTING.'

'But—'

'Oh, Amelia, please! I don't have time for this! I have a million things to do before the performance tomorrow, programmes to run up, caterers to meet with. I really don't care to stand here and argue with you about it. You two are kissing, and that's final. Unless you want me to have a word with a certain chorus member—'

I threw a panicky look in Amber Cheeseman's direction. I'm stuck. And Grandmere knows it.

Which might be why she was wearing a smug little smile on her face as she stormed off to wake up Señor Eduardo and send him home.

As if all that weren't bad enough, though, when I walked out the doors of the hotel just now and started towards the limo, J.P. stepped out from the shadows and said my name.

'Oh,' I said, all confused. I mean, had he been waiting for me? Well, obviously. Only . . . why? 'What's wrong? Do you need a ride home? We can drop you off if you want.'

But J.P. was like, 'No, I don't need a ride. I want to talk to you. About the kiss.'

!!!!!!!!!!!!!

OK. So THAT didn't freak me out too much.

But I couldn't show it or anything, because Lilly was in the limo waiting for me, and she totally saw us there

242

on the red carpet and put the window down and was like, 'Come on, you two, I have to get home and collate!'

God, she can be annoying sometimes.

'Look, Mia,' J.P. said, completely ignoring Lilly, as was only fitting. 'I know you're having problems with your boyfriend, and that they're partly because of me – no, don't try to deny it. Tina already told me. I was really worried about you, because you just looked so down all day, so I forced it out of her. So, listen. We don't have to kiss. Once we're up there during the performance, we can pretty much do what we want, anyway. I mean, it's not like your grandmother would be able to stop us. So, I just wanted to tell you – if you, you know, don't want to, we don't have to. I won't be offended or anything. I totally understand.'

OH MY GOD!

Isn't that the sweetest thing you ever heard in the whole world?????

I mean, it's just so thoughtful and mature and unlike me of him!

I think that's why I did what I did next:

Which was stand up on my tiptoes and kiss the Guy Who Hates It When They Put Corn In The Chilli on the cheek.

'Thank you, J.P.,' I said.

J.P. looked extremely surprised.

'For what?' he asked in a voice that cracked a little. 'All I said was that you don't have to kiss me if you don't want to.'

'I know,' I said, giving his hand a squeeze. 'That's why I kissed you.'

Then I jumped into the car.

Where Lilly was immediately all over me with

questions, since we were dropping her off on our way to the loft.

Lilly: 'What was that about?'

Me: 'He said I didn't have to kiss him.'

Lilly: 'Then why did you? Kiss him, I mean?'

Me: 'Because I thought he was sweet.'

Lilly: 'Oh my God. You like him.'

Me: 'Just as a friend.'

Lilly: 'Since when do you kiss your guy friends? You've never kissed Boris.'

Me: 'Ew. Did you hear what he said that one time about being an over-saliva secretor, or whatever it was? I don't know how Tina stands it.'

Lilly: 'What is going on with you two, Mia? You and J.P.?'

Me: 'Nothing. I told you, we're just friends.'

And the thing is, even though I knew I shouldn't go there, because Lilly is about to receive the worst news she's ever had, in the form of her parents breaking up – I mean, when someone finally gets around to telling her, and all – I totally went there. Because I was just so mad.

244

Me: 'The real question is, what's going on with YOU
           and J.P.?'

Lilly: 'ME? *I*'m not the one who kissed him. Or sexy
           danced with him. I just like him as a friend, like
           you CLAIM you do.'

Me: 'Then why won't you pull the story I wrote about
           him from your 'zine? I mean, you know it's just
           going to hurt his feelings. If you really like him
           as a friend, why would you want to hurt him?'

Lilly: '*I* won't be the person hurting him. *You* will.
           I didn't write that story.'

God. Why does she have to rub it in?

Wednesday, March 10, Midnight, the Loft

No emails from Michael.

No messages either.

I realize he has a lot on his mind right now, and can't be like totally focused on me and MY needs. I wasn't expecting to come home and find a big bouquet of roses with a note tucked in them that said *I love you*.

But a phone call reassuring me that we are, in fact, still going out might have been nice.

Yeah. So didn't happen. I came home and everyone in the house was already asleep. Again.

Being an actress, dedicated to her craft, is no joke. I mean, now I know how Meryl Streep must feel, stumbling home at all hours of the night after rehearsing whatever Academy Award-winning movie she's in. I will never again think that acting is an easy career to have.

Anyway, I am taking Tina's advice, and Giving Michael Some Space. The way she does with Boris when he has to learn some new Bartók.

And I can't say I really blame Michael for not calling or e-ing me, since I'm obviously not the most *stable* person he knows. I don't know what I was thinking, trying to prove I was a party girl when I'm so not. Basically, I was just trying to manipulate Michael, and that is never a good idea. I mean, unless you're Grandmere or Lana, who are masters at the art of manipulation – particularly the manipulation of the laws of supply and demand.

But that doesn't mean it's right.

Seriously. Just because you CAN do something well doesn't mean you SHOULD do it.

Like my short story, for instance. I mean, sure, I can write.

But does that give me the right to write a story based on someone who actually exists, who might possibly read that story and get upset about it?

No. Just because you HAVE the power doesn't mean you should USE it. Or, at least, ABUSE it.

Which is what Grandmere and Lana do, with the whole economics thing. If you are lucky enough to HAVE a talent – like mine, for writing – you have a moral obligation to use that talent for GOOD.

That's what happened at the party. You know, when I did the sexy dance? That's why it backfired. Because I was trying to manipulate people. Which is evil, not good.

I'm an evil economics abuser. I'm –

SOMEONE IS IMing ME!!!!!!!!!!

LET IT BE MICHAEL

LET IT BE MICHAEL

LET IT BE MICHAEL

LET IT

Oh. It's Lilly.

WomynRule: You know, it was really presumptuous of you to have kissed him if you don't even like him that way. What if he gets the wrong idea? You already sexy danced with him, and now you're going around kissing him? For someone so worried about hurting his feelings, you sure don't seem to have thought that through.

!!!!!

FtLouie: Oh, yeah? Well, for someone who
            claims not to like him as anything
            but a friend, you sure do seem con-
            cerned about him liking me.
>
WomynRule: Only because I THOUGHT you were
            dating my brother. But apparently
            one guy's not enough for you. You
            have to have ALL the guys.
>
FtLouie: WHAT??? What are you talking about?
            I DO NOT LIKE J.P.
>
WomynRule: Sure you don't. I bet if I looked
            at your nostrils right now, they'd
            be flaring.
>
FtLouie: OMG, I am NOT lying. Lilly, I love
            your brother, and ONLY your
            brother. You KNOW that. What is
            WRONG with you?
>
WomynRule: Terminated

Wow. It's a good thing her parents aren't telling her
about their separation just yet. If this is how she acts
when she DOESN'T know about it, I hate to think how
she's going to act when she DOES.

Unless she DOES know, like Michael suspects, and
she's just PRETENDING she doesn't know. That would
explain a lot about her current behaviour.

But, regardless, at least I know what I have to do now. My mission is, at last, clear. A feeling of calm has descended over me.

Oh, wait, that's just Fat Louie, sleeping on my feet.

Still. I have a plan.

About how I'm going to keep J.P. from reading 'No More Corn!', I mean. I don't know what I'm going to do about the rest of the mess that is my life.

But I know what I'm going to do about *Fat Louie's Pink Butthole*.

And, truthfully, I think Carl Jung AND Alfred Marshall would approve.

From the desk of
Her Royal Highness Princess Amelia Mignonette
Grimaldi Thermopolis Renaldo

Dear Dr Carl Jung,

Hi. Sorry about my last letter. I was kind of . . . you know . . . cuckoo.

Well, you know all about that. I mean, you devoted your entire career to the study of psychos like me.

Anyway, just wanted to say not to worry. Things are better now. I think I finally get it. You know, the whole transcendence thing. It's not about what's happening INSIDE you. It's what you put OUT that matters.

Well, not, you know, *put out* like sex. But I mean what you put out into the universe. It's about being kind to others, and telling the truth instead of lying all the time, and using your powers for good and not evil. Like, if your boyfriend is having a party, you should just go and try to have a good time, instead of resorting to elaborate schemes to try to make him think you're a party girl.

And if your friend is going to run a story in a magazine that could really hurt someone's feelings, you should stop her.

Right?

Anyway, I'm seriously going to devote the rest of my

life to the Telling the Truth and Doing Good Works. I really mean that. Because I know now that that's the only way I'm going to achieve self-actualization, and that people like my grandmother and Lana Weinberger, who resort to lies and blackmail and abuse the law of supply and demand, will never find spiritual enlightenment.

Anyway, seeing as how I have now pledged to walk the Path of Truth and all that, do you think there's a chance that part of my self-actualization, when it comes after I perform all my good works, could be getting my boyfriend to forgive me for being such a freak? Because I seriously miss him.

I hope that's not asking too much. I honestly don't mean to be selfish. It's just, you know. I love him and all.

Hopefully,
Your friend,
Mia Thermopolis

Wednesday, March 10, Homeroom

So, Lilly isn't speaking to me, apparently. She wasn't waiting outside her building this morning for us to pick her up and take her to school. And when I ran inside to buzz her apartment, no one answered.

But I know she's not at home sick, because I saw her just now outside Ho's Deli, buying a soy latte.

When I waved, she just turned her back.

So now BOTH the Moscovitzes are ignoring me.

This is not a very nice way to start my first day on the Path to Righteousness.

Wednesday, March 10, PE

OK, so I know skipping gym is probably not the most direct path to achieving transcendence from the ego.

But it's for a totally good cause!

Even Lars thinks so. Which is convenient, since I'm going to need his help carrying the stuff. I mean, I don't have the upper-body strength to lift 3,700 pieces of paper.

At least, not all at once.

Wednesday, March 10, US Economics

OK. So I guess I still have a ways to go on the Path to Righteousness.

I mean, I really THOUGHT I was doing the right thing.

At first.

I totally remembered Lilly's locker combination from the time she got the flu and I had to take her her books.

And when I opened her locker door, the stack of 1,000 copies of *Fat Louie's Pink Butthole*, Volume 1, Issue 1, was just sitting right there, waiting to be sold today at lunch.

It was so easy to grab them.

Well, OK, not THAT easy, because they were heavy. But Lars and I split the pile between us, and I was frantically looking around for a place to hide them – some place Lilly would never find them, because you so know she's going to look – when I spied the men's room.

Well, come on! How's she going to look for them there?

So Lars and I staggered in there, with these giant armfuls of paper, and I barely had time to register the fact that in the men's room at AEHS there is no mirror over the sinks, and also no doors on the bathroom stalls (which is completely sexist if you ask me, because don't boys need to see how their hair looks and privacy too?), before I realized we were not alone in there.

Because John Paul Reynolds-Abernathy the Fourth was standing at one of the sinks, wiping his hands on a paper towel!!!!!

'Mia?' J.P. looked back and forth from Lars to me. 'Um, hey. What's up?'

Both Lars and I had frozen. I went, 'Um. Nothing.'

But J.P. didn't believe me. Obviously.

'What's all that?' he asked, nodding at the huge stacks of papers we were each sagging under.

'Um,' I said, desperately trying to think of some kind of excuse I could give him.

Then I remembered I'm supposed to be treading the Path of Truth and all, and I had pledged to the memory of Dr Carl Jung that I wouldn't lie any more.

So I had no choice but to say, 'Well, the truth is, these are copies of my short story for *Fat Louie's Pink Butthole*, which I stole out of Lilly's locker and am trying to hide in the men's room, because I don't want anyone to read them.'

J.P. raised his eyebrows. 'Why? You don't think your story's any good?'

I REALLY wanted to say yes.

But since I swore I'd tell the truth from now on, I was forced to say, 'Not exactly. The thing is, I wrote this story, um, about you. But way before I had ever met you! And it's really stupid and embarrassing, and I don't want you to read it.'

J.P.'s eyebrows went up even MORE.

But he didn't look mad. He looked – actually, he kind of looked like he was kind of flattered.

'You wrote a story about me, huh?' He leaned against one of the sinks. 'But you don't want me to read it. Well, I can see your dilemma. Still, I don't think hiding them, even in the men's room, is going to work. She's bound to get someone to look in here, don't you think? I mean, it's the first place *I'*d look, if *I* were Lilly.'

The thing was, after he said it, I knew he was right. Hiding the copies in the men's room wasn't going to keep Lilly from finding them.

'What else can we do with them?' I wailed. 'I mean, where can we put all this so she won't find it?'

J.P. appeared to think about this for a moment. Then he straightened up and said, 'Follow me,' and walked past us, back out into the hallway.

I looked at Lars. He shrugged. Then we followed J.P. out into the hall, where we found him pointing . . .

. . . at one of the recycling bins. One of the ones I'd ordered, that said, 'Paper, Cans and Battles' on it.

My shoulders sagged with disappointment.

'She'll totally look there,' I wailed. 'I mean, it even says PAPER on it.'

'Not,' J.P. said, 'if we put it all in the crusher.'

Which was when he tossed the paper towel he'd used to dry his hands into the can section of the recycling bin . . .

Which immediately sprang to life and began its crushing action, smushing the paper towel to shreds.

'Voila!' J.P. said. 'Your problem is solved. Permanently.'

But as the recycling bin's internal crushing device finally quieted down, I looked down at the stack of magazines in my arms.

And knew that I couldn't do it. I just couldn't. As much as I hated that horrible cover, and the story I'd written beneath it, I knew I couldn't destroy something Lilly had worked so hard on.

'Princess?' Lars shifted his arm-load of magazines and nodded towards the hallway clock. 'The bell is about to ring.'

'I –' I looked from the pinkly glowing magazine cover to J.P.'s face, then back again. 'I can't do it. J.P., I'm sorry. But I just can't. She would be so hurt . . . and she's going through a really tough time right now. Even if she doesn't know it.'

J.P. nodded.

'Hey,' he said. 'I understand.'

'No,' I said. 'I don't think you do. My story about you is really stupid. I mean, REALLY stupid. And everyone is going to read it. And know that it's about you. Which I admit makes ME look like the fool, not you. But people might . . . you know. Laugh. When they read it. And I really don't want to hurt your feelings any more than I want to hurt Lilly's.'

'I wouldn't worry too much about me,' J.P. said. 'I'm a loner, remember? I don't care what other people think of me. With the exception of a select few.'

'Then . . .' I nodded at the pile of magazines in my arms. 'If I put these back where I found them, and Lilly sells them at lunchtime, you won't care?'

'Not a bit,' J.P. said.

And he even helped Lars and me stuff them all back into Lilly's locker.

Then the bell rang, and everyone started pouring out into the hallway and going to their lockers, and so we had to say goodbye or we'd have been late to our next class.

The saddest part is, Lilly will never know the sacrifice J.P. is making on her behalf. He TOTALLY likes her. It's so OBVIOUS.

Wednesday, March 10, English

Hey, are you nervous about tonight? Our big debut?
I know I am!

> To tell you the truth, I haven't really had a chance to
> think about it.

Really? Oh my gosh - you still haven't heard from
Michael?

> No.

Probably because he's going to surprise you with a
big bouquet of roses after the performance tonight!

I wish I lived in Tinaland.

Wednesday, March 10, Lunch

I walked into the caff, and there she was. At the booth she set up, underneath all these signs she'd made, advertising today's sale of the first issue of the school's new literary 'zine.

I knew I had to be, you know. Nice about it. On account of Lilly's home life being unsatisfactory. Or going to become that way, anyway, even if she didn't quite know it yet.

So I went up to her and was like, 'One copy, please.'

And Lilly went, all businesslike, 'That will be five dollars.'

I totally couldn't help myself. I was like, 'FIVE DOLLARS??? ARE YOU KIDDING????'

And Lilly went, 'Well, it's not cheap putting out a magazine, you know. And you were the one harping on about how we have to make back the money we blew on the recycling bins.'

I coughed up the five bucks. But I had my doubts it would be worth it.

It wasn't. Besides my story and Kenny's dwarf thesis, there were a couple of mangas, one of J.P.'s poems, and . . .

. . . all five of the short stories Lilly wrote for the *Sixteen* magazine contest. Five. She put FIVE of her own short stories in her magazine!

I could hardly believe it. I mean, I know Lilly thinks pretty highly of herself, but—

It was right then that Principal Gupta walked in. She NEVER comes into the cafeteria. Rumour has it that she once stepped on a Tater Tot someone dropped and it grossed her out so much she would never set foot in the caff again.

But today she crossed the caff and, heedless of any Tater Tots that might have been underfoot, went right up to Lilly's booth!

'Uh-oh,' Ling Su, next to me, said. 'Looks like someone's busted.'

'Maybe Gupta objects to the cover illustration,' Boris suggested.

'Um, I think it's more likely she's objecting to this story Lilly wrote,' Tina said, holding up her copy. 'Did you guys READ this? It's totally nc-seventeen!'

I hadn't actually read any of Lilly's stories. She'd just told me about them. But even a rudimentary scan through them showed me that –

Oh, yes. Lilly was very, very busted.

All copies of *Fat Louie's Pink Butthole* were being confiscated by Coach Wheeton, who had brought a large black trash bag for that purpose.

'This is a violation of our right to free speech!' Lilly was shouting as Principal Gupta escorted her from the caff. 'People, don't just sit there! Get up and protest! Don't let the man keep you down!'

But everyone just sat where they were, chewing. Students at AEHS are totally used to letting the man keep us down.

When Coach Wheeton, spying the copy of Lilly's magazine in my hands, came up to me with his trash bag and went, 'Sorry, Mia. We'll see that you get your money back,' I dropped it in.

Because what else could I do?

J.P. and I just looked at each other.

I wasn't sure whether or not it was my imagination, but he seemed to be LAUGHING.

I'm glad SOMEONE can see something funny in all this.

Then Tina took me aside . . .

'Listen, Mia,' she said softly. 'I didn't want to say anything in front of the others, but I think I just figured something out. I read this romance novel once where the heroine and her evil twin were both in love with the same guy, the hero. And the evil twin kept doing all this stuff to make the heroine look bad in front of him. The hero, I mean.'

'Yeah?' What did this have to do with me? I wondered. I don't have a twin.

'Well, you know how you kept asking Lilly to pull "No More Corn!", and she wouldn't do it, even though she knew it would hurt J.P.'s feelings and all, if he read it?'

What was she getting at? 'Yeah?'

'Well, what if the reason Lilly refused to pull your story was because she WANTED J.P. to read it. Because she knew if he read it, he'd get mad at you for writing it, and then he wouldn't like you any more. And then he'd be free to like HER instead.'

At first I was like, 'No way. Lilly would never do something like that to me.'

But then I remembered the final thing she said to me during last night's limo ride home from the Plaza:

'*I* won't be the person hurting him. *You* will. *I* didn't write that story.'

Oh my God! Could Tina be right? Does Lilly like J.P., but thinks he likes me? Could that really be why she was being so stubborn about pulling 'No More Corn!'?

No. No, that can't be right. Because Lilly doesn't GET all weird and possessive about boys. She just doesn't.

'I'm not saying she was doing it CONSCIOUSLY,' Tina said when I mentioned this. 'She probably hasn't even admitted to HERSELF that she likes J.P.. But, SUBCONSCIOUSLY, this could be the reason why she refused to pull your story.'

'No,' I said. 'Come on, Tina. That's crazy.'

'Is it?' Tina wanted to know. 'Think about it, Mia. What HASN'T Lilly lost to you lately? First the school presidency. Then the part of Rosagunde. Now this. I'm just saying. It would explain a lot.'

Well, it *would* explain a lot. If it were true. But it's not. J.P. doesn't like me that way, and Lilly doesn't like HIM that way.

And even if she did, she would never do something like that to me. I mean, she's the person I love seventh best in the whole world. And I'm sure she loves me third. Or maybe fourth. On account of her not having a boyfriend, a younger sibling, a bodyguard, or any pets of her own.

Wednesday, March 10, G and T

Lilly's back. She's looking really pale. Apparently, Principal Gupta called her parents.

Who came in to school. For a conference.

I don't know what they talked about. At the conference, I mean. But, apparently, Lilly has to run the content of the next issue of *Fat Louie's Pink Butthole* past Ms Martinez before she's allowed to sell it. Because Lilly never showed Ms Martinez her short stories.

Or mine.

Or the name of the magazine. Which is being changed to *The Zine*.

Just *The Zine*.

Which is, as I told Lilly in an effort to be kind, kinda catchy.

Lilly didn't say anything back to me like, 'Thanks,' or, 'I'm sorry.'

And I'm not saying anything to her like, 'Want to talk?' or, 'I'm sorry.'

But I wish I could.

I'm just afraid of what she'll say back.

Wednesday, March 10, Third-floor stairwell

Today must be some kind of record for me breaking school rules. Because Kenny and I just totally skipped Earth Science, and we're up here with Tina, going over the choreography one last time before tonight's performance.

Kenny says he's so nervous he wants to throw up. Tina too.

Me? To tell the truth – and it's my personal mission in life to ONLY tell the truth any more – I could vomit up my intestines, I'm so freaked out.

Because tonight I am going to have to do something I have never done before in my life. And that's kiss a boy.

A boy other than Michael, I mean.

Well, OK, except for Josh Richter, but he doesn't count, because that was before Michael and I started going out.

But basically, tonight I am going to cheat on my boyfriend.

And OK, I know it's not really cheating, since it's just a play – I mean, musical – and we are only acting a part and don't really like each other or anything.

But still. I'll be kissing ANOTHER MAN. A man I, only last Saturday, sexy danced with. In front of my boyfriend.

Who didn't like it very much. So much so, in fact, that he's apparently not speaking to me now. So if he finds out about this kissing thing, I'm REALLY going to be dead.

And even if he doesn't find out, *I WILL KNOW*.

How can I help but feel like I am betraying him somehow?

Especially if – and this is what worries me most – I end up LIKING it. Kissing J.P., I mean.

Oh, God. I can't believe I even WROTE that.

Of COURSE I won't like it. I only love one boy, and that's Michael. Even if he doesn't necessarily love me back right now. I could NEVER enjoy kissing someone else. NEVER.

Oh, God. WHY WON'T HE CALL?????

Wednesday, March 10, The Big Performance

He still hasn't called.

And there are so many people here.

I'm serious.

I can't actually see who any of them are because Grandmere won't let us peek out from behind the curtains, because she says, 'If you can see the audience, they can see you.' She says it's unprofessional to be seen in costume until after the show has started.

Considering this is an amateur production, Grandmere sure is a stickler about us all acting professional.

Still, I can see there are like twenty-five rows of chairs, with like twenty-five seats across out there, and every seat is filled. That's like . . . five thousand people!

Oh, no, wait. Boris says it's only six hundred and twenty-five.

Still. That is a LOT of people. Not ALL of them can be related to us, you know? I mean, obviously, there are CELEBRITIES out there. According to Netscape, which I checked just before I left for the Plaza, Grandmere's Aide de Ferme benefit is sold out – donations for the Genovian olive growers have been pouring in all week from movie stars and rock musicians alike. Apparently, Grandmere's benefit – with its musical tribute to Genovian history – is THE place to be tonight.

I could be totally wrong, but I think I saw Prince – the artist formerly known as Prince, I mean – demanding an aisle seat just now.

And what about the REPORTERS? There are a ton of them, crouched down behind the orchestra, their cameras poised to photograph us the minute the curtain goes up. I can just see tomorrow's headline emblazoned across the *Post*: *PRINCESS PLAYS A PRINCESS*. Or worse, *PRINCESS TAKES A BOW*.

Shudder.

With my luck, they'll get a picture of J.P. and me kissing, and THAT will be the photo they pick for the front page.

And Michael will see it.

And then he'll TOTALLY break up with me.

OK, I am such a shallow person, worrying about my boyfriend breaking up with me, when he is currently going through what is probably the most painful personal crisis of his life and so clearly has way bigger things to be concerned about than his dumb high-school girlfriend.

And why am I even worrying about this when I am supposed to be focusing on my performance? According to Grandmere, anyway.

Everyone backstage is REALLY nervous. Amber Cheeseman is in the corner, doing some hapkido warm-up moves to calm down. Ling Su is doing breathing exercises she learned in her yoga class at the Y. Kenny is pacing around, muttering, 'Step-ball-change. Step-ball-change. Jazz-hands, jazz-hands, jazz-hands. Step-ball-change.' Tina is helping Boris run through his lines. Lilly is just sitting quietly by herself, trying not to mess up her costume's long white train.

Even Grandmere has broken her own rules again and is smoking, despite the fact that her last meal was hours ago.

Only Señor Eduardo seems calm. That's because he's asleep in a chair in the front row, with his equally ancient wife dozing beside him. They were the only two people I recognized before Grandmere caught me peeking.

Two minutes until the curtain goes up.

Grandmere has just called us over to her. She puts out her cigarette and says, 'Well, children. This is it. The moment of truth. Everything you've worked so hard for over the past week has been leading up to this. Will you succeed? Or will you fall on your faces and make fools of yourselves in front of your parents and friends, not to mention any number of celebrities? Only you can decide. It's entirely up to you. But I've done all I can for you. I've written what is, perhaps, one of the finest musicals of all time. You can't blame the material. Only yourselves, from this point on. Now it's your turn, children. Your turn to spread your wings, as I have – and fly! Fly, children! FLY!'

Then she says, into the walkie-talkie none of us has noticed she's carrying until that very moment, 'For God's sake, it's seven o'clock, start the overture now.'

And the music begins . . .

Wednesday, March 10, The Big Performance

Oh my God, they LOVE it! Seriously! They're eating it up! I've never heard a crowd applaud so hard! They are going NUTS! And we haven't even got to the finale yet!

Everybody is doing SO well! Boris hasn't forgotten any of his lines – he sang the Warlord song perfectly:

> Going out to kill and slay
> Is what I do every single day
> No other job would I request
> Marauding is what I do best!
>
> *Chorus:*
> Riding through forests in the night
> When I emerge it's quite a sight
> In villagers' eyes, it's fear I see
> Oh, what a blast it is to be me!

And Kenny hasn't messed up any of the choreography. Well, OK, he has, but not enough so anyone would notice.

And you could have heard a pin drop when Lilly sang the Mistress's song!

> How was I to know
> When to him my mother sold
> Me, that one day I would grow
> To love him so?
>
> Though all he does is rape and plunder
> To me it's always been a wonder
> That when he's done with pillaging
> It's me he turns to for his loving.

She held that crowd in the palm of her hand! Her voice THROBBED with poignancy, just like Madame Puissant taught her! *And* she remembered only to use one hand while lifting up her train to climb the stairs.

J.P. practically got a standing ovation for his Smithy song.

> How could someone like she
> Ever love a poor man like me?
> When clearly she could have anyone
> Why would she settle for this someone?
>
> How could she
> Ever love me?

And the song right before I strangle Boris was so POWERFUL!!!! You could hear people in the audience – the ones who are unfamiliar with Genovian history – gasp when I sang the line, 'So with this braid, I make the turn/Around his neck, so he may burn.' Seriously.

> Though twilight brings this day to close
> What comes tomorrow none can know.
> I lie here in this bed of hate
> And look to night to cast my fate . . .
>
> *Chorus:*
>
> Father, Genovia, together we will fight!
> Father, Genovia, for the future is tonight!
>
> Cross my heart and hope to die,
> My father's death I'll avenge, swore I.

So with this braid I make the twist
That by morning's light he'll not exist!

And when I sang that second chorus of 'Father, Genovia, together we will fight! Father, Genovia, for the future is tonight!' I am almost positive I heard Grandmere – GRANDMERE, of all people – sniffle!

Well, OK, maybe she's just suffering from a bit of post-nasal drip. But still.

Oh, it's time for the big finale! This is it. Time for the big kiss.

I really hope Tina isn't right and J.P. doesn't like me that way. Because no matter what happens, my heart belongs to Michael and always will.

Not that kissing someone else in a play – I mean, musical – is like cheating on him. Because it totally isn't. What J.P. and I—

Where IS J.P. anyway? We're supposed to hold hands and run out on to the stage together, with looks of joy upon our faces, and then he gives me the big kiss.

But how can I hold his hand and run out on to the stage when he's MISSING????

This is crazy. He was here after the last number. Where could he—

Oh, finally, here he comes.

Wait – that's someone in J.P.'s costume. But that's not J.P. . . .

Wednesday, March 10, The Big Party

Oh my God. I can't believe ANY of this is happening.

Seriously. It's all like a dream. Because when I reached out to grab J.P.'s hand and rush out on to the stage with him, I found myself grabbing MICHAEL's hand, instead.

'MICHAEL?' I couldn't help exclaiming. Even though we aren't supposed to talk backstage, on account of our body mikes possibly picking it up. 'What are you—'

But Michael put his finger to his lips, pointed to my mike, then grabbed my hand and dragged me out on to the stage –

Exactly the way J.P. had, in all our rehearsals.

Then, as everyone sang, 'Genovia! Genovia!' Michael, in J.P.'s Gustav costume, swept me into his arms, bent me back, and planted the biggest movie kiss you've ever seen on my lips.

Nobody even noticed it wasn't J.P. until the curtain call, when we all had to grab hands and bow.

'*Michael!*' I cried again. 'What are you doing here?'

We didn't have to worry about our mikes picking anything up at that point, because the audience was clapping so hard, they wouldn't have heard it anyway.

'What do you mean, what am I doing here?' Michael asked with a grin. 'Did you really think I was going to stand idly by while you kissed another guy?'

Which was right when J.P. walked past us and went, 'Hey, man. Good one,' and held out his palm, which Michael lightly slapped.

'Wait,' I said. 'What's going on here?'

Which was when Lilly stepped up and draped an arm around my neck.

'Oh, POG,' she said. 'Chill out.'

Then she went on to describe how she and her brother – with J.P.'s help – concocted this plan to have Michael and J.P. switch places during the finale, so Michael, not J.P., could be the one who kissed me.

And that's precisely what they did.

How they managed to do so behind my back, though, I will never know. I mean, seriously.

'Does this mean you forgive me for the sexy dance thing?' I asked Michael after we'd been de-miked and de-braided and we were alone in one of the wings back-stage, while off stage everyone else was getting congratulated by their family – or meeting the celebrity of their dreams.

But what did I need with celebrities, when the person I looked up to most in the world was standing RIGHT THERE IN FRONT OF ME?

'Yes, I forgive you for the sexy dance thing,' Michael said, his arms tight around me. 'If you'll forgive me for having been such an absentee boyfriend lately.'

'It's not your fault. You were upset about your parents. I totally understand.'

To which he replied simply, 'Thanks.'

Which made me realize, then and there, that being in a mature relationship has nothing to do with drinking beer and dancing sexy. Instead, it has everything to do with being able to count on someone not to break up with you just because you danced with another guy at a party one night, or not to take it personally when you can't call them as often as you'd like because you're super busy dealing with midterms and a family crisis.

'I'm really sorry, Michael,' I said. 'I hope things will work out for your parents. And, um, seriously . . . about what happened at your party – the beer – the beret – the sexy dance. None of it will ever happen again.'

'Well,' Michael admitted. 'I did sort of enjoy the sexy dance.'

I goggled up at him. 'You DID?'

'I did,' Michael said, leaning down to kiss me. 'If you promise me that next time, you'll do it just for me.'

I promised. Did I EVER.

When Michael finally lifted his head for air, he said, his voice a little unsteady, 'The truth is, Mia, I don't want a party girl. All I've ever wanted is you.'

Oh. So THAT'S what he'd been going to say.

'Now, what do you say we go take these stupid costumes off,' Michael said, 'and join the party?'

I said I thought that sounded just fine.

Wednesday, March 10, Still the Big Party

They are giving speeches now. The developers of The World, I mean. Which, it took me a minute to remember, is why Grandmere was having this party in the first place. NOT to raise money for the Genovian olive farmers, or even to put on a play. I mean, musical.

This whole thing was to butter up the people in charge of deciding who gets what island.

I can't say I envy them – the people in charge, I mean. How do you decide who deserves Ireland more: Bono or Colin Farrell? How do you decide who should get England: Elton John or David Beckham?

I guess ultimately it all boils down to who pays the most money. Still, I'm glad I don't have to be the one to make the decision if, say, they refuse to bid any higher.

One thing I KNOW has been decided is who gets Genovia. THAT was pretty obvious when J.P., looking totally red-cheeked and sheepish, was dragged over to where I was standing near Grandmere by a huge balding man, smoking a cigar.

'There she is!' the huge balding man – John Paul Reynolds-Abernathy the Third, I quickly realized, J.P.'s dad – exclaimed. 'The little lady I've been dying to meet, the Princess of Genovia, the one responsible for bringing my boy here outta his shell! How're ya, sweetheart?'

I thought J.P.'s dad must have been talking about Grandmere. You know, since she was the one who'd cast J.P. in her show, which could, I guess, be considered 'bringing him out of his shell'.

But to my surprise, I saw that Mr Reynolds-Abernathy the Third was gazing down at ME, not Grandmere.

Grandmere, for her part, was looking as if she smelt something foul. Probably it was the cigar.

But all she said was, 'John Paul. This is my granddaughter, Her Royal Highness Princess Amelia Mignonette Grimaldi Thermopolis Renaldo.' (Grandmere always reverses my last two names. It's a thing between her and my mom.)

'How do you do, sir,' I said, sticking out my right hand . . .

Only to have it swallowed up in Mr Reynolds-Abernathy the Third's big, meaty paw.

'Couldn't be better,' he said, pumping my arm up and down, while J.P., standing next to his dad with his hands buried deep in his pockets, looked like he wanted to die. 'Couldn't be better. I'm pleased to make the acquaintance of the girl who – sorry, *princess* who – is the first person at that stuck-up school you kids go to ever to ask my boy to lunch!'

I just stood there, looking from J.P. to his dad and then back again. I sort of couldn't believe it. I mean, that no one at AEHS had ever asked J.P. to join them for lunch before.

On the other hand, he *did* say he wasn't much of a joiner. And he WAS always really weird about the corn in the chilli thing. And if you didn't know the story behind why . . . well, you might think he was kind of strange. Until you got to know him better, I mean.

'And look what it's done for him!' Mr Reynolds-Abernathy the Third went on. 'One little lunch and the kid's got the lead in the school musical! And he's even got friends now! College friends! What's that one guy's name, J.P.? The one you were talking to all last night on the phone? Mike?'

J.P. was looking steadfastly at the floor. I didn't blame him.

'Yeah,' he said. 'Michael.'

'Right, Mike,' Mr Reynolds-Abernathy the Third went on. 'And the princess here.' He gave me a chuck under the chin. 'Kid's been eating lunch alone since he started at that snobby school. I was gonna make him transfer if it went on much longer. Now he's eating lunch with a princess! It's the damnedest thing. That is one fine granddaughter you've got there, Clarisse!'

'Thank you, John Paul,' Grandmere said graciously. 'And may I say, your son is a very charming young man. I am sure he will go very far in life.'

'Damned right he will,' Mr Reynolds-Abernathy said, and now it was J.P.'s turn to get a chuck under the chin. 'Eating lunch with princesses. Well, just wanted to say thanks. Oh, and to let you know I withdrew my bid for that island – what's it called? Oh, right! Genovia! "Together we will fight." Love that line, by the way. Anyway, right, it's all yours, Clarisse, seeing the favour your little granddaughter did for me and my boy here.'

Grandmere's eyes nearly popped out of her head. So did Rommel's, on account of she was squeezing him so hard.

'Are you quite certain, John Paul?' Grandmere asked.

'One hundred per cent,' Mr Reynolds-Abernathy the Third said. 'It was a mistake for me to bid on it in the first place. I never wanted Genovia – though it took me seeing this play tonight to realize it. It's that other one, the one with the car race—'

'Monaco,' Grandmere suggested coldly, looking like she smelt something even worse than cigar smoke. But then, she ALWAYS looks like that when she's reminded of Genovia's closest neighbour.

'Yeah, that's the one.' J.P.'s dad looked grateful. 'I gotta remember that. Buyin' it for J.P.'s mom, you know, for an anniversary present. She loves that movie star, the one who was princess there, what's her name?'

'Grace Kelly,' Grandmere said in an even colder voice.

'That's the one.' Mr Reynolds-Abernathy the Third grabbed his son by the arm. 'C'mon, kid,' he said. 'Let's go put a bid in, before one of these other, er, *people* –' He was full on staring at Cher, who did have a pretty skimpy outfit on, but was still human and all '– snap it up.'

As soon as they were out of earshot, I turned to Grandmere and said, 'OK, admit it. The reason you put on this play was NOT to entertain the masses who would come to donate money to the Genovian olive growers, but to ingratiate yourself with J.P.'s dad and get him to drop his bid on the faux island of Genovia, wasn't it?'

'Perhaps initially,' Grandmere said. 'Later, I will admit, I rather got into the spirit of the thing. Once bitten by the theatre bug, it remains in the blood you know, Amelia. I will never be able to turn my back completely on the dramatic arts. Especially not now that my show –' She glanced in the direction of all the reporters and theatre critics who were waiting for her to make a statement '– is such a hit.'

'Whatever,' I said. 'Just answer one question for me. Why was it so important to you that J.P. and I kiss at the end? And tell me the truth for a change, not that bunk about the audience expecting a kiss at the end of a musical, or whatever.'

Grandmere had shifted Rommel in her arms so that

she could examine her reflection in the diamond-encrusted compact she'd pulled from her bag. 'Oh, good heavens, Amelia,' she said, checking that her make-up was perfect before she went to be interviewed. 'You're not yet sixteen years old, and you've only kissed one boy in your entire life.'

I coughed. 'Two, actually,' I said. 'Remember Josh—'

'Pfuit!' Grandmere said, closing her compact with a snap. 'In any case, you're much too young to be so serious about a boy. A princess needs to kiss a lot of frogs before she can say for certain she's found her prince.'

'And you were hoping John Paul Reynolds-Abernathy the Fourth would turn out to be my prince,' I said. 'Because, unlike Michael, his dad is rich . . . and also happened to be bidding against you for the faux island of Genovia.'

'The thought did cross my mind,' Grandmere said vaguely. 'But what are you complaining about? Here's your money.'

And just like that, she handed me a cheque for exactly five thousand, seven hundred and twenty-eight dollars.

'The money you need for your little financial problem,' Grandmere went on. 'It's just a small percentage of what we've actually raised so far tonight. The Genovian farmers will never know it's missing.'

My head spun. 'Grandmere! Are you serious?' I didn't have to worry any more about Amber Cheeseman sending my nasal cartilage crashing into my frontal lobe! It was like a dream come true.

'You see, Amelia,' Grandmere said smugly. 'You helped me, and I helped you. That is the Renaldo way.'

This actually made me laugh.

'But *I* got you your island,' I said, feeling a bubble of triumph – yes, *triumph* – well up inside me. 'I asked J.P. to eat lunch with me, and that's what made his dad drop his bid. I didn't have to stoop to any elaborate lies or blackmail schemes or strangulation – which appears to be the Renaldo way. But there's another way, Grandmere. You might want to check it out. It's called being *nice* to people.'

Grandmere blinked down at me.

'Where would Rosagunde have got, if she'd been *nice* to Lord Alboin? Niceness, Amelia,' she said, 'gets you nowhere in life.'

'*Au contraire*, Grandmere,' I said. 'Niceness got you the faux island of Genovia, and me the money I needed . . .'

And, I added silently to myself, *my boyfriend back* . . .

But Grandmere just rolled her eyes and went, 'Does my hair look all right? I'm heading over to the photographers now.'

'You look great,' I told her.

Because what does it hurt to be nice?

As soon as Grandmere had been swallowed up by the press corps that had been waiting for her, J.P. appeared, holding out a glass of sparkling cider for me, which I took from him and gratefully gulped down. All that singing can make you thirsty.

'So,' J.P. said. 'That was my dad.'

'He seems to really love you,' I said diplomatically. Because it wouldn't have been nice to say, *God, you were right! He IS super embarrassing!* 'In spite of the corn thing.'

'Yeah,' J.P. said. 'I guess. Anyway. Mad at me?'

'Mad at you?' I cried. 'Why are you always asking if I'm mad at you? I think you're the greatest guy I ever met!'

'Except Michael,' J.P. reminded me, glancing over to where Michael stood, having a heart-to-heart with Bob Dylan . . . not far, actually, from where Lana Weinberger and Trisha Hayes were being ignored by Colin Farrell. And pouting because of it.

'Well, of course,' I said to J.P. 'Seriously, that was SO SWEET, what you did for me . . . and for Michael. I honestly can't thank you enough. I don't know how I'll ever be able to repay you.'

'Oh,' J.P. said with a smile. 'I'm sure I'll think of something.'

'I do have one question though,' I said, finally getting the guts to ask him something that had been bothering me for a while. 'If you hate corn so much, why do you even GET the chilli? I mean, in the caff.'

J.P. blinked at me. 'Well, because I hate corn. But I love chilli.'

'Oh. OK. See you tomorrow,' I said, and gave him a little wave goodbye. Even though I didn't understand at all.

But, you know, I've pretty much come to the conclusion that I only understand about fifteen per cent of what people are saying to me, anyway. Like what Amber Cheeseman said to me a little while ago, over by the caviar bar: 'You know, Mia, you're really fun in person. After all the stuff I've read about you, I expected you to be sort of a stick-in-the-mud. But you're a real party girl after all!'

So, I guess the definition of 'party girl' sort of varies, depending on who, you know, is doing the talking.

A second later, Lilly sidled up to me. If I hadn't known the truth – you know, about her parents – I might have been all, 'Lilly! What are you doing, sidling up to people? You don't sidle.'

But since I knew from the sidle that she knew the truth about them now – nothing else could have made her seem so sad – all I said was, 'Hey.'

'Hey.' Lilly was gazing across the room at Boris, who was pumping Joshua Bell's hand so hard it was clear he might actually break it. Behind him stood two people who could only be Mr and Mrs Pelkowski, both beaming shyly at their son's hero, while behind THEM, my mom and Mr Gianini, and Lilly's parents, were listening intently to something Leonard Nimoy was telling them. 'How's it going?'

'All right,' I said. 'Did you get to talk to Madonna?'

'She didn't show,' Lilly said. 'I had a nice chat with Colin Farrell though.'

I raised my eyebrows. 'You did?'

'Yeah,' Lilly said. 'He agrees with me that the IRA needs to be disarmed, but has some pretty radical ideas on how they ought to go about doing it. Oh, and then I had a long talk with Paris Hilton.'

'What did you and Paris *Hilton* talk about?'

'Mostly the peace process in the Middle East. Though she did say she thought my shoes were hot,' Lilly said.

And we both looked down at Lilly's black Converse high-tops, the ones she'd drawn silver Star of Davids all over, in order to celebrate her Jewish heritage, and which she'd donned especially for tonight's occasion.

'They *are* nice,' I admitted. 'Listen, Lilly. Thanks. For helping to straighten out things between me and Michael, I mean.'

'What are friends for?' Lilly asked, with a shrug. 'And

don't worry. I didn't tell Michael about that kiss you gave J.P.'

'It didn't mean anything!' I cried.

'Whatever,' Lilly said.

'It didn't,' I insisted. And then, because it seemed like the right thing to do, I added, 'Look. I'm really sorry about your parents.'

'I know,' Lilly said. 'I should have – I mean, I've known for a while things weren't going so well for them. Morty's been moving away from the neo-psychoanalytical school of psychiatry ever since he left grad school. He and Ruth have been fighting over this for years, but it all came to a head with a recent article in *Psychoanalysis Today*, blasting the Jungians for essentialism. Ruth feels Morty's attitude towards the neo-psychoanalysis movement is merely a symptom of a midlife crisis and that, next thing you know, Morty'll be buying a Ferrari and vacationing in the Hamptons. But Morty insists he's on the verge of an important breakthrough. Neither of them will back off. So Ruth asked Morty to move out until he gets his priorities back in order. Or publishes. Whichever comes first.'

'Oh,' I said. Because I couldn't figure out how else to respond. I mean, do couples really split up over things like this? I've heard about people getting divorced because one person keeps on losing the cap to the toothpaste.

But to break up over methodological differences?

Oh, well. At least that's one I never have to worry about happening to Michael and me!

'Still, I shouldn't have kept it all to myself,' Lilly went on. 'I should have told you. At least it might have helped you understand – you know. Why I've been acting like such a freak lately.'

'At least,' I said gravely, 'you have an excuse. For freakish behaviour, and all. What's mine?'

Lilly laughed, the way I'd meant her to.

'I'm sorry I wouldn't pull your story,' she said. 'You were totally right. It would have been mean to J.P. Not to mention completely insulting to your cat.'

'Yeah,' I said, glancing over to where J.P. was standing, not too far from Doo Pak, who was breathlessly telling Elton John something. 'J.P.'s a really nice guy. And you know –' Well, why not? The niceness thing hadn't let me down yet – 'I think he really likes you.'

'Shut up,' Lilly said. But not in quite as listless a voice as she'd been speaking in before. 'I've given up guys. You know that. They don't bring anything but trouble and heartache. It's like I was telling David Mamet a minute ago, that—'

'Wait,' I said. '*David Mamet* is here?'

'Yeah,' Lilly said. 'He's buying the faux island of Massachusetts or something. Why?'

'Lilly,' I said excitedly. 'Go up to J.P. and tell him you want to introduce him to someone. Then take him over to David Mamet.'

'Why?'

'Don't ask. Just do it. I swear you won't regret it. In fact, I bet he asks you out afterwards.'

'Do you really think he likes me?' Lilly wanted to know, eyeing J.P. uncertainly.

'Totally,' I said.

'Then I'm going to do it,' Lilly said, with sudden determination. 'Right now.'

'Go for it,' I told her.

And she went.

But I didn't get to see how J.P. reacted, because at that very moment Michael came up and slid an arm around my waist.

'Hi,' I said. 'How was Bob?'

'Bob,' Michael said, 'is so cool. How are *you*?'

'You know what? I'm good.'

And I wasn't even lying, for a change.

Ten out of Ten

Princess Amelia Mignonette Grimaldi Thermopolis Renaldo (Mia)

invites you to an exclusive event to celebrate her 18th birthday and the FABULOUS last ever instalment of The Princess Diaries

Dress code: Glamorous and gorgeous. Tiaras optional. And, Lana Weinberger, don't forget your underwear!

Etiquette: No curtsying. No paps. No kissing Prince William.

Mia's princess training is almost over. She can climb out of a limo as elegantly as any European heir presumptive. Even Grandmere approves of her practically perfect boyfriend, J.P. So this is the final instalment, the very end, the last EVER entry in The Princess Diaries. After all, Mia's about to turn eighteen – it's time to leave childish things behind. Like:

1. Lying.
2. Therapy with Dr Knutz – Mia's so ready to move on!
3. Being Albert Einstein High's last and only unicorn*.
4. Thinking about Michael Moscovitz. I mean, come ON. He's in Japan. And, besides, Mia is TOTALLY in love with J.P.
5. Michael who?

* You have *so* got to read the book!

air head

meg cabot

She's a brainiac trapped inside the body of an airhead ...

Teenagers Emerson Watts and Nikki Howard have nothing in common. Em's a tomboy-brainiac who couldn't care less about her looks. Nikki's a stunning supermodel; the world's most famous airhead. But a freak accident causes the girls' lives to collide in the most extraordinary way – and suddenly Em knows more about Nikki's life than the paparazzi ever have!

The first book in a spectacular, romantic trilogy with a spine-tingling twist!

ABANDON

MEG CABOT

PIERCE KNOWS WHAT IT'S LIKE TO DIE.

Last year she flatlined following an accident.

During that time Pierce saw a dark world and
met a mysterious, irresistible boy.

Now that boy, John Hayden, has turned up at school.
Every time she sees him Pierce finds herself in
terrible danger. Yet she's still drawn to him.

John wants to take her back to the place she
fears the most: the Underworld.

The question is, why?